I0787991

THE LAST DAY
OF
CAPTAIN LINCOLN

Library of Congress Control Number: 016907864

ISBN 978-0-9975902-5-8 (Hardcover)
ISBN 978-0-9975902-8-9 (Paperback)

www.EXOBooks.com

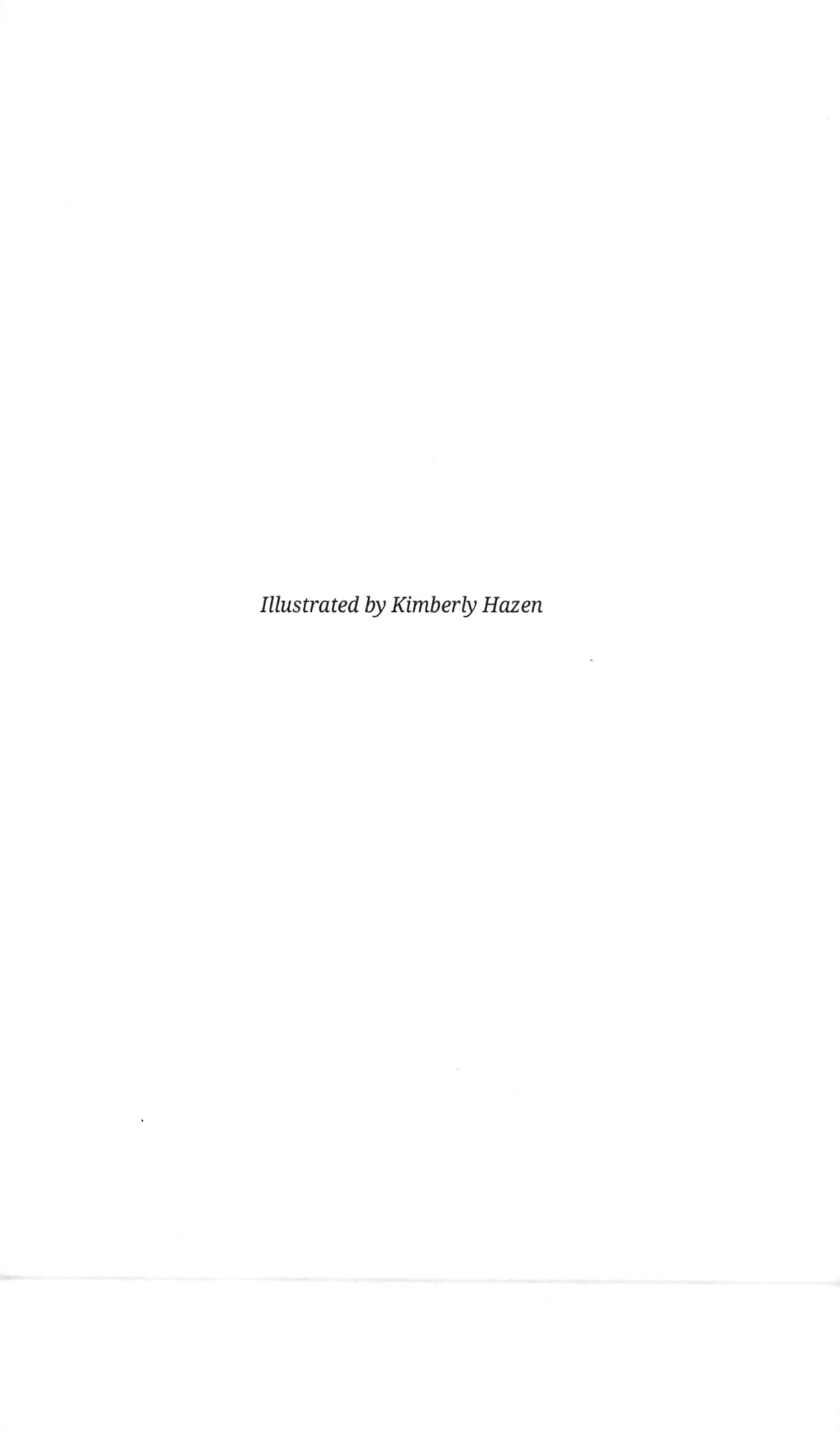

Illustrated by Kimberly Hazen

Listen to the cry of a woman in labor
at the hour of giving birth—look at
the dying man's struggle at his last
extremity, and then tell me whether
something that begins and ends thus
could be intended for enjoyment.

Søren Kierkegaard
Deceased 11 November 1855 AD (aged 42)
Copenhagen, Denmark, Earth

ONE

All our knowledge merely helps
us to die a more painful death than
animals that know nothing.

Maurice Maeterlinck
Deceased 6 May 1949 AD (aged 86)
Nice, France, Earth

The U.S.N.A.S. *Hope Eternal* hung at the edge of a new solar system after an interstellar exodus that had lasted thousands of years. The spaceship was tucked into a safe orbit, in the furthest-out asteroid belt of the second star ever visited in-person by actual human beings. Even so far out, the radiation from the massive red sun caused the gunmetal skin of the ship to glisten as if it were wet, casting the perfectly-round orb as the jewel among the meteoroids and frozen volatiles which made up the rest of the wide asteroid belt.

From the perspective of the huge star dominating the system the Ship was nothing: a puny, worthless object, just like the countless others helplessly locked in orbit around the great, life-giving, God.

From the perspective of the Ship (and all 128 souls on board) something was very, very wrong.

The sun was humongous: a hundred times bigger than it ought to have been, and a thousand times brighter. The immense brilliance basked the two gas giants of the system with an almost unholy glow. The closer gassy planet burned a fiery, eternally-angry red, while the one further out shimmered a thoroughly opaque yet slightly more hopeful blue. Both of the giant planets were ringed by bright silver discs which reflected decadently in the extra light, further adding to the effect; the two great balls of gas greedily hoarding most of the dust hemorrhaging out of the Solar System.

The inner planets weren't faring so well. The three rocky planets supposed to be closest to the swollen sun were not even there, devoured in various flaming hells eons ago. The fourth planet—*allegedly* an idyllic blue marble perfect for *Earth 2.0* (and still awaiting a suitable new name from the first people to set down on it)—was actually further away than it should have been in orbit. That hadn't saved it. *Earth 2.0* was a depressing shade of burnt-out brown, nothing more than a worthless, barren ashtray of cinder and dust.

"Captain!" It was the voice of Warren, one of the youngest crewmembers on the Command Deck. The urgency and fear in her voice instantly cut through the fog of silence. "I don't even know where to start… Literally everything is wrong."

Captain Lincoln stood there, deathly serious, his arms crossed over his crisp red uniform shirt. He was directly under the circular dome at the center of the large Command Deck, near the core of the dense Ship. The perimeter of the room was manned by men and women sitting at various (at this point almost entirely useless) posts. And right now they were all helplessly staring at their leader.

"Put something onscreen at least …," growls Lincoln. "Share with the rest of the class." Yet his choice of words bounds away, engulfed and forgotten in the tense silence that instantly returns.

A large part of the dome above suddenly became alive, flashing with all sorts of scrolling readouts and 3-D graphs. Several more colorful, multi-layered screens on the walls also come to life.

"Warren!" orders Lincoln. "Translate this for us."

"That's the problem, Sir," the promising young girl replies. "Every single reading is anomalous." She shakes her head in amazement. "This just can't be, Sir."

"Sir . . . ," another woman begins, seamlessly taking up the fumbled baton yet her voice also quivering with fear. "This star is totally unstable. The core is far too cool. Even though it looks gigantic, it's actually *lost* most of its original mass. Spectral analysis shows that there is virtually no hydrogen or helium left—only a thin shell on the outside. The interior is nothing but carbon. Nuclear reactions have all but stopped."

Lincoln realized that he couldn't move. His bottom half was paralyzed, his naked feet rooted to the floor of the Control Deck—totally not by his command.

"Are any of the other probes working?" asks Lincoln in a low voice.

"No, sir," a man directly behind him answers. "The only probe sending any readings is *Angel*, the oldest. She was the first released before we began deceleration. She also happens to be the furthest one out, parked 6.3 AUs from the star."

"Do we have a visual feed from her?"

"Yes sir."

A large portion of the front wall switches to the probe's camera feed and suddenly the whole scene is directly in front of them, in ultra hi-definition. The massive red sun was clearly far larger than it should have been, engulfing almost all of the screen. A monstrous cloud of gas and dust encircled it like a hazy cocoon.

"Sir, this star is . . . well it's already dead—it just

doesn't know it yet," says Warren. This time she was far more composed. "How is this even possible, though?"

Lincoln shook his head slowly but no words could come out of his mouth. At that moment his feet released their grip on the floor. Finally he could move his legs again, but hovering there just inches over the floor he had absolutely no way to control his momentum or direction. His arms and legs shot out spastically, each on their own accord; instinctively trying to stall for time and orientate for the fall which might come any second.

"Captain!" someone cries, border-line hysterical. "What are your orders?"

"Oh, Captain!" someone else cries. "What do we do, Sir?"

A stream of thoughts raced desperately through Lincoln's mind but underneath it all he knew that nothing could be done. They were helpless.

"CAPTAIN!" the walls rumble with the ultra-deep voice of the Ship. "Another large pulse is coming. Indeed, this one may be the last. Solar collapse appears to be imminent."

Lincoln closes his eyes as he takes a deep breath, attempting to focus his attention. It doesn't work. When he opens his eyes, the red star taking up most of the screen is shivering like a hive of angry bees. Then, in a tremendous flash of light a ring of gas blasts out from the convulsing star, hurtling forth in every direction at once. A moment later the visual feed cuts out, leaving the black and white snow of dead air hanging on the screen.

"Captain!?!" A crew member cries. "What do we do?" Hysterical, the fear gripping his voice demands an answer to the utterly hopeless question. "WHAT DO WE DO?" he pleas again.

Lincoln sighs deeply, just about the only thing he could do, enjoying two final, measured breaths for himself before he speaks calmly to all of the people around him. "I'm sad to say it, but ladies and gentlemen we are out of time."

His eyes helplessly scan the crew as the room slowly seems to rotate around him, like he was the sun and they were his beautiful planets.

"There's absolutely nothing we can do about this, people. Prepare yourselves the best you can. It was a pleasure to know, and serve, with each of you. I love you all very much."

Time seemed to slow in the next few agonizing moments, while a strange noise began to build. It sounded like a hypersonic ambulance was bearing straight for them, the quivering wail becoming higher and higher in pitch as it quickly approached. Then the Ship began to shake, a tremor which soon grew into a bone-rattling earthquake.

Swiveling his head around, taking in the faces of his friends one last time, all Lincoln could see was the fearful horror distorting their normally beautiful features. The lights cut out and the room went black, silent for a single moment more.

There's nothing I can do about it! was the very last thought to pierce his mind.

Then came the explosion, ending with a searing, high-pitched white light which shot straight through his brain.

* * *

Lincoln woke with a start. Underneath his blanket his naked body was drenched in sweat. He didn't smell particularly good, either. To his right he saw that Helen, thankfully, was still next to him. Under the starlight her beautiful face was relaxed in the tranquil peace of deep sleep.

It was dark and quiet except for their breathing. The only light in their small room came from the starscape shining from the ceiling, as usual, but when he focused on the stars directly above him he noticed that something was different. The scene had been taken from the North America skies almost a millennium ago, but one of the brightest stars that had always been there was now gone, replaced with a slowly expanding donut of blue and fiery red, the center empty and black. It was remarkably beautiful in one respect, but the change was unsettling too, rekindling the unease from his nightmare.

Lincoln shook his head as he exhaled, still jarred from the dream.

Sliding out of bed, his naked body stung for a second as it adjusted to the cooler air programmed for nighttime on the Ship. Exhaling a tad too loudly, Lincoln glanced backwards. Helen rolled over, as if turning on cue, her body unconsciously feeling for his. Too late to go back, with a shake of his head he continued to the hygiene station in the corner of the room. He drew a tube out from the middle of the wall and took a drink of cool water.

The stars had always been the default setting for the ceiling when they were kids. It was one thing that Lincoln had never really messed with when he got older, either. Being under the stars gave him a feeling that somehow combined wonder and peacefulness. The vast, silent, twinkling beauty of a clear night sky, combined with the knowledge of what the stars really were—and thinking about what that could represent—was usually a good antidote for centering a soul.

Not today, though.

Peering into the mirrored wall in the corner, Lincoln leaned close to examine his face. The gentle starlight made him look much younger than his eighty Earth-standard years, masking the lines of wear around his face and hiding a bad case of red, tired eyes.

"Not so bad still, old man," he growled softly, with the crooked grin he'd stolen from some long dead actor. Truth be told, Lincoln would pass for an extremely fit forty-five or fifty-year-old Earthling. This was apparent, of course, because the entirety of Earth's media had been uploaded into the Ship before it had blasted away. Lincoln's healthy appearance was due to a veritably stress free life, a nutritionally-optimized vegetarian diet sourced from the farms on the Ship, real time medical monitoring though several pieces of implanted technology, and, perhaps most importantly, his own superior genetic design. Lack of sleep and too much alcohol, both of late, were only just beginning to take their toll.

Lincoln had always liked the classic, *Old America* movies the best, from the couple of decades before the true apex of the Second Age (along with a lot of the music of the time, too); admiring the noble Jimmy Stewart, and the Westerns of John Wayne. From the dawn of his own consciousness onward, he'd naturally gravitated towards the strong, silent type. True to both taste and form, the steady dark eyes of the reflection staring back at him concealed the turbulent emotions shaking him to the core.

You see, today was to be Captain Lincoln's last: to be specific, his 29,220ᵗʰ day aboard an interstellar starship currently hurtling between Earth and another still very far-away star. And he was tired. Tired deep down … a profound tiredness that had settled deep within his bones. He'd spent much of the past few months contemplating his own impending demise only to frustratingly realize that this time would've been better spent in a hundred different ways. Time, after all, was the enemy. The ultimate bogeyman. Always there, whenever you looked. *Time is money! There's no time to lose! The time to act is now!* And Lincoln had frittered away so much of his own precious time in a quest for answers that hadn't resulted in much—especially a cure for the pangs once again tormenting his stomach, twisting it in knots.

"Lincoln—get your ass back in bed!"

Helen's voice shot across the room, pulling him back into the here and now with a tone more insistent than anything he'd ever heard from her before. He looked back at her, not happy that any part of his bout of vanity had been spotted. He was surprised by her tone but he decided he liked it, and so he obeyed. He came back to bed quickly, smoothly slipping his arm under her neck as he lay back down. The blanket moved on its own accord, silently rippling as it covered his body too.

Helen put her head onto his chest. "Lincoln," she

whispered. "You've been so distant these last few days ... far away in some other place instead of here with me. Where have you been, my love?"

Her eyes demanded an answer, but it took some time for them to work a reply.

"That's a tough question," he finally offered.

"Come on, Link," she urged, tenderly running her fingers through the thick patch of silver and black hair covering his chest. "Today is a hard day for everybody. It's the only hard day, really. But instead of spending your time with me you pulled away. What have you been looking for?"

She tugged on the hair when he didn't answer.

"It's a hard day for me too, you know," she said, her voice barely a whisper.

Lincoln closed his eyes, a reflex perhaps, as he struggled with the emotions that once again began to bubble up from deep within. It must have been three or four of her slow breaths before he answered, in a low sing-song voice, his eyes still closed:

> *God knows 'twere better to be deep*
> *Pillowed in silk and scented down*
> *Where love throbs out in blissful sleep,*
> *Pulse nigh to pulse, and breath to breath,*
> *Where hushed awakenings are dear...*
> *But I've a rendezvous with Death.*[1]

Lincoln sighed before he opened his eyes.

"This rots. There's no better way to say it than that. Philosophically, it makes sense—I'm old. Logically, it makes sense—I need to die. It's my time and we need to make room for young ones." He shook his head. "But it still doesn't sit easy, that's for sure. I was extremely sad when the Epsilon Omegas were reclaimed, but when it's you, your own death? You know, I actually asked the Ship for a diagnosis a couple of weeks ago. The answer?"

Lincoln prompted the Ship to answer through the walls.

"Clinical depression, Captain," it said in a woman's voice, with just the touch of some exotic accent.

"Yeah," Lincoln continued with a nod. "I was depressed. I guess I still am. There was this woman on Earth who believed that there were five stages to dying.[2] It doesn't really seem to fit though. Maybe it's something from Earth society that I don't get. Denial? No. There's no denying the fact that I am going to die. Isolation? Obvious enough. I've been isolating myself, as you say. Anger? At who, or what? The Ship? Our society? Then Bargaining. Again—with who? The Ship? Should I beg for new babies not to be born? The very last step is acceptance, but that's a giant case of easier said than done. I can't say that I have."

He sighed again.

"That's the easy explanation: it's hard grappling with your own death. I've been searching for a bigger meaning to it all—life and death and everything in between, an inherently tough proposition even with the right questions."

Lincoln slowly ran his hand through her thick hair as he looked at the stars above them. The halo from the supernova had expanded even further now, beginning to blot out many of the stars around it as it continued to grow in size.

"Rationalization is a fine thing—it's really easy. Plain and simple, the Ship can only support so many people. That's a built in, acute payload problem that appeals to any Captain's mind—with the only answer being an easy one decided long ago. Eighty years is a fine life too, the eighty fully guaranteed, with no illnesses to speak of. And it's a great eighty years because we're given everything we could ever need. Any human being ever born would probably take that deal . . . "

Pausing mid-stream, Lincoln shook his head at his lover.

"But it still fucking rots. No matter of rationalization changes the fact that I want to lay in bed with you for at least another twenty years."

Lincoln turned his body, twisting from underneath her while keeping her close, so that they lay face-to-face on their sides.

"I'm sorry that I've been so distant, Helen. It took me a long time to realize it, and I love you for understanding, but … I just couldn't control myself. It's like a switch in my brain was flipped on—*impending doom mode*, everything flashing in red—and I couldn't turn it off. Even now."

Indeed, according to the Ship's clinical diagnosis Lincoln's depression began about six months ago, during a regular lunch with the current Captain, Captain Kennedy, and a few other of the more venerable retired crew members. The first mention of the initial preparations for today's Lustrum Birthday Feast had taken Lincoln totally by surprise. That night his sleep problems began. They never stopped.

Lincoln squeezed Helen tight.

"You're absolutely right, *mi amor*. I got stuck in there, pulled in a hundred different directions in my own head, very far away from you and all of the other people who love me. You know what finally snapped me out of it? *The last uploads of Captain Adam.* I'd read most of his work multiple times already, but the last time just resonated so much more. It was an epiphany—I finally got it. Here is a man whose life was so different than ours. Alpha generation was the very first generation of *Homo evolutis* … the first people to be born off of Earth. Here's a man who grew up in a community with Earthlings as they endeavored to create our Ship, literally inventing and then building all the technology that keeps us safe and alive and so happily occupied! Captain Adam is *the* Captain of the *Hope Eternal* as she blasts away from Earth … and when he dies they're just barely out of the Solar System!"

"Still, at the end, despite all of these differences between us, Captain Adam was asking the exact same questions I've been asking this whole time. But by all accounts, dying should've been easier on him. They'd just set out on this grand adventure. They had such a strong sense of purpose back then too, a purity of belief we no longer remember because we're too comfortable, so happily and obliviously self-occupied that we forget the frightening speed at which we're hurtling through space. But Captain Adam also had the same issues I've been having. He couldn't sleep at the end. He couldn't eat, either. He felt guilty because, deep down, acute payload problem and all, he didn't want to die. Not at all. Not one bit."

Lincoln paused, thinking about it all again.

"Listening to his words, feeling the exact same feelings, it helped pull me out of the worst of my own depression. Captain Adam showed me that it's natural to fear death, as a conscious, thinking being—it's the literal end of you. I'm not even afraid of death itself. It's more of a profound … not wanting to leave the party. So, I managed to stop dwelling on it all—at least on the conscious level. The real problem is the sub-conscious. I wish there was a way to turn it off. Some things still work though…"

He began to kiss her on the neck.

"Lincoln …," she laughed musically, "do you re-member our first time?"

He pulled back, smiling his crooked smile. "Of course I remember!"

They had met in the farms during a harvest. Lincoln was fifteen years older than her and Helen was only just a woman. Unabashed, she'd asked Lincoln to make love to her five times over the course of those first few months before he finally agreed to it. There was actually *Ship protocol* regarding the situation (which wasn't known to young ones until after the fact), requiring that the older person wait until at least the third inquiry before even thinking about accept-ing. This was in view of human history and physiolog-ical changes in the human body, but mostly designed to protect against the caprice of youth. Though every-one on the Ship was sterile and sex was shared freely and often—*the gift of love*—it was a strict rule in a so-ciety with few others.

"Short hair … gawky girl." Lincoln's smile grew wider and wider as he spoke. "Very little fashion sense of any kind! And I had always been attracted to older women. They were so…mysterious—uninhibited and wild. You were not like that at all. At least not yet!" he laughed.

Lincoln finished smoothly with a sly smile. "We did seem to click, though."

Helen faked her outrage pretty convincingly. "We did, but only after you actually started to talk to this *gawky girl*! You're infuriating, you know that? I was attracted to you instantly."

She sized him up with a mischievous smile.

"Tall, dark, and handsome. Certainly the *sturdy* phenotype—well-proportioned and muscular. You know what though, Captain? I really think it could've been that hideous beard you wore back then that had triggered my first infatuation with you. You're quite the hairy ape, you know that Mister? Well, opposites attract, as the old saying goes. According to this ancient wisdom that happens to make your particular body design subtly and inexplicitly irresistible to most of the women onboard this Ship—and a few of the men."

Once again Helen slowly ran her hand through the thick patch of hair covering his chest. The pleasure of her soft touch caused him to close his eyes with a content smile.

"Everyone knows the power that a woman's tits and ass can have on a man—you fellas haven't exactly been bred to be discreet. But in just about every culture I've studied the women preferred their men to be taller than them, with darker skin and hair as well. The evidence completely backs up the old *tall, dark and handsome* thing. You just said it yourself…evolution has imbedded a very strong subconscious into the human brain—a literal mind of its own. And my particular brain was preprogrammed to find a tall, dark, hairy, muscular man like you supremely attractive."

Helen smiled her own devastating smile.

"Lincoln, my dear … You must know this by now. You may think you're so smart and dashing, but the real reason we women always found you so attractive is because you're one extremely beautiful specimen of caveman."

"HAH!" Lincoln cracked. "Eloquent, my dear—as always. Sadly, that pretty much explains everything… "

"So, why'd you do it, then?" she asked. "You could have—let's face it—you *have* had just about every woman you've wanted on this Ship. Why'd you say yes to me, Link? Skinny, gawky, old me?"

Lincoln considered his words thoughtfully before he spoke, knowing it was a time for a serious answer.

"Even that young I knew that you were very special. Somehow, you captivated me—not an easy thing for a young girl to do to a man, outside of the bedroom. We talked and talked and talked and I never grew bored. You asked questions that no one else ever asked. We were interested in many of the same things. And we laughed. We laughed a lot."

He paused for a second, struck by a memory.

"Do you remember Bonduca?"

Helen nodded, refreshing the picture in her memory by pulling up the woman's file on a screen imbedded in her eye. Bonduca, Epsilon Chi, had been a bodily-kinesthetic experimenting in dance-driven martial arts when Helen had first seen her as a girl. The picture in her mind was of a bold, powerful older woman fiercely leading one group against another in a vigorous tournament of various fighting skills. The video certainly backed that up.

"She was why I said no, at first...," Lincoln continued. "We were together at the time. When I told her about you she wasn't happy, to say the least. She became very possessive after that—a trait that quickly wore thin. We're all allowed to be selfish once in a while, but it is a terrible trait in any quantity. Still, it really made me think about things—me and her, you and me—and I'm sure glad for it now. It adds up to right here, right now, and that's a very good thing."

He laughed as he slapped her ass, giving it a meaty squeeze for good measure. "And you didn't turn out to be a slouch yourself."

They smiled at each other happily, in the moment.

"You know," Helen began cautiously, "it's been

very hard watching you struggle. My first instinct was to come rushing to you. To scream in your face, to shake you out of it… anything to get you to come back to me. But I knew that you needed to take the time on your own. We all have a different journey, Lincoln. Life is not about robotically applying what you think you've learned, whether it's from *Captain Adam's Last Uploads* or anywhere else."

Helen emphasized her words.

"Even now, it may all still seem unfathomable to you, Captain Lincoln, but your particular trip isn't done just yet. Remember that true enlightenment is never finished. Ever. Understanding is never complete."

She smiled gently at him. "And I am here for you, my love, for whatever you need, until that time."

Lincoln smiled back.

"You are an amazing woman. I have never doubted that."

"I love you, Captain Lincoln."

"I really love you, Helen. Truly. Thank you… Thank you for everything."

Lincoln didn't feel like talking anymore so he kissed her deeply. Sucking on her bottom lip, he twisted his body while urging hers down, so that she could feel his full weight pressing on top of her. She liked it. Relenting to the advance this time, Helen responded with her entire body. One of her hands grabbed his neck while the other was in the hair on the top of his head. Her legs wrapped around him.

Soon they began to make love again (for the record, the fourth time of the evening). It was long and slow, in no rush for anything. Lincoln was the one to trigger the music that began playing through the walls, choosing the graduated build of Boléro, long a personal favorite for moments such as this:

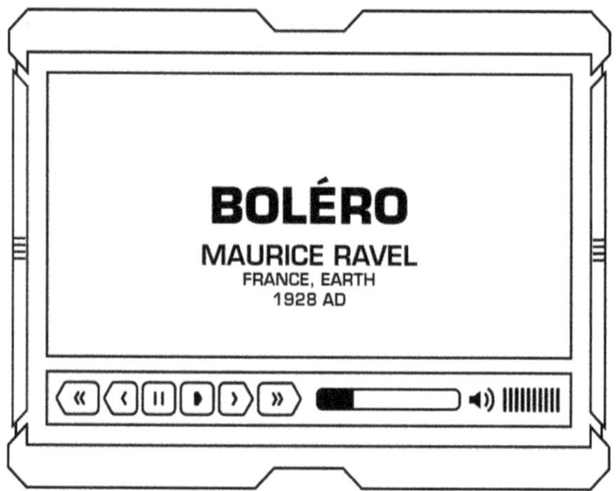

Later, when their love making peaked, it was near the climax of "their" song, toggled on by Helen at just about the perfect time:

Talk about saving the best for last.

From a letter to his brother Theo

9 July 1888 AD

That brings up again the eternal question: is life completely visible to us, or isn't it rather that this side of death we see one hemisphere only?

Painters — to take them only — being dead and buried, speak to the next generation or to several succeeding generations through their work.

Is that all, or is there more besides? In a painter's life death is not perhaps the hardest thing there is.

For my own part, I declare I know nothing whatever about it. But to look at the stars always makes me dream, as simply as I dream over the black dots representing towns and villages on a map. Why, I ask myself, shouldn't the shining dots of the sky be as accessible as the black dots on the map of France? Just as we take a train to get to Tarascon or Rouen, we take death to reach a star. We cannot get to a star while we are alive any more than we can take the train when we are dead.

So to me it seems possible that cholera, tuberculosis and cancer are the celestial means of locomotion, just as steamboats, buses and railways are the terrestrial means. To die quietly of old age would be to go there on foot.

Vincent Van Gogh
Deceased 29 July 1890 AD (aged 37)
Auver-sur-Oise, France, Earth

TWO

We say that the hour of death
cannot be forecast, but when we
say this we imagine that hour as
placed in an obscure and distant
future. It never occurs to us that
it has any connection with the
day already begun or that death
could arrive this same afternoon,
this afternoon which is so certain
and which has every hour filled in
advance.

Marcel Proust
Deceased 18 November 1922 AD (aged 51)
Paris, France, Earth

When Lincoln woke Helen was gone. He didn't like that very much. Artificial sunlight sudden ly flooded down from the ceiling, making the room unbearably bright. He swung his legs over and sat on the edge of the bed—still feeling as tired as ever—as he waited for his eyes to adjust to the light. Lincoln sat for a good minute, relaxing in the quiet—until he checked the time.

It was 9:47 am.

"Shit, you asshole!" he swore out loud. "Last day alive and you oversleep."

Stark naked, when Lincoln's feet touched the black floor the dark walls of the small room suddenly transformed with a swirl of colors into a dazzling landscape. As he padded towards the hygiene station, a majestic sunrise enveloped the room, his bed now under a steadily growing blue-yellow sun on the shore of a bright azure sea. The landscape was covered with a strange, autumnal rainbow of plant life; mostly yellows and oranges and reds all throughout the vast tropical jungle, which grew almost to the tops of the purple mountains ringing the other end of the room.

The title of the piece automatically flashed in front of his eyes as he walked:

Yet Lincoln didn't even notice the art around him. Using his eye implants he launched several applications at once, the most immediate being the rock and roll starting out of the walls. At the hygiene station he pulled out a tube from lower on the wall, flipped the top open and began to take a piss.

He'd always preferred external audio the best. It just sounded better than playing it in your ears. You could *feel* the bass ... in your bones—just like you're supposed to. Music is about an emotional connection and playing it through the walls made it feel more like you were there, in the same room as the performers. This particular song was spooky though: starting with a simple guitar line, then a gun-shot snare and unsettling bass, all hauntingly relentless.

Still pissing, Lincoln pulled up the credit:

"Seriously?!? Are you going to fuck with me all day?"

One could communicate with the Ship in any number of ways. In an empty room, considering recent actions and tone of voice, the Ship correctly deduced that Lincoln was addressing it.

"Captain—you know that I would not *fuck* with you."

The sonorous voice that rung in Lincoln's ears was a woman's, in an exotic accent that had probably once started as British. Unlike the stars always on the ceiling, Lincoln had changed the Ship's *private* voice to him many, many times over the course of his life. Lately he'd settled on the sexy alto for their private communications.

"What's this song about?" said Lincoln. "Not a great choice for today …all things considered."

The Ship's answer was close to instantaneous (it being the greatest computer ever known to have been created in the Universe), but it delayed it for a moment. According to experience, people didn't like getting the answer before their question was finished.

"Seemingly depression, directly manifested from the death of a partner," the voice said. "So sorry, Captain. That came from a random algorithm. We can do much better."

Another song began, much more upbeat than the first.

When he finally finished his first order of business, Lincoln stepped into the narrow shower tube. The door sealed with a pneumatic hiss. Lincoln barely fit, with only a very small space left at the top and his arms uselessly clinging to his sides—one small penal-

ty for being bigger than most. He closed his eyes and mouth, holding his breath while the tube rapidly filled up with the water-based cleaning solution.

Using the implants in his eyes, he saw that he had a message from his sister, Sojourner, making sure that Lincoln would be meeting with the rest of his siblings for their private party later in the day. Lincoln sent off a quick reply: *Yes, my love.* With ten seconds to go in the thirty second cycle, he pushed his arms and legs against the outside of the tube as much as it allowed—there's nothing worse than showering and not getting the shit out of all of your nooks and crannies. The tube drained quickly, followed by the fast drying cycle of warm, charged air. Lincoln stepped out smelling like daisies.

He flicked on an application to review the day's schedule. It was jam-packed, with absolutely no time to spare:

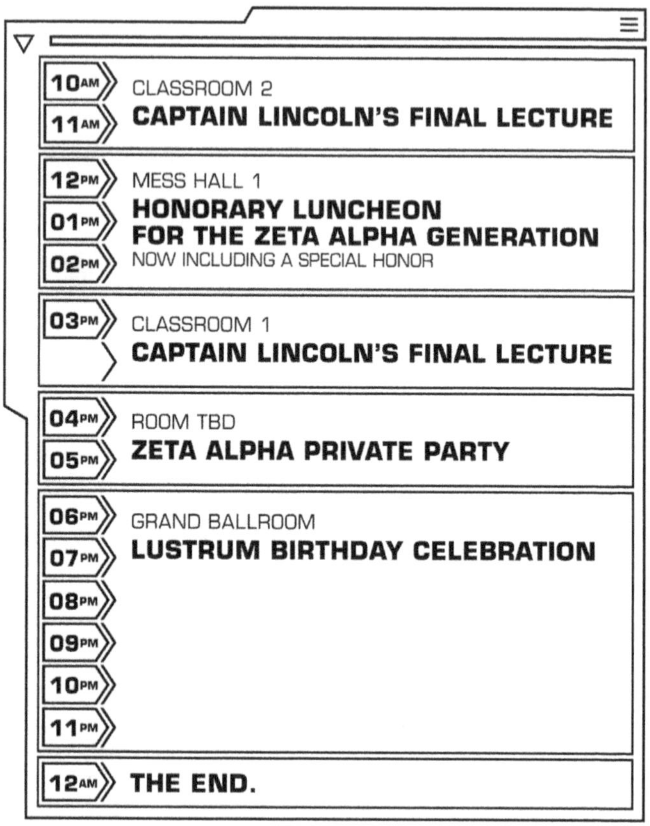

To be clear, Lincoln was no longer *The* Captain. He was an older, retired Captain; for just a little while longer the oldest statesmen of the group, thus therefore a bit of a dignitary. But it's not like Captains directed the Ship at this juncture of the voyage (or anyone, for that matter). The Ship's course, engine cycles and general functionality were all determined ages ago. The elected Captain was regarded as a leader and general role model though, and old Captains retained that respect, with speaking roles at certain functions and performance of other casual duties long after the conclusion of their official terms. The title held great prestige, tracing back hundreds of years to their first, dear, Captain Adam. Lincoln certainly appreciated the history as well as the honor and prestige, but the absolute best part of the job of Captain was being a mentor and friend to the children.

Today was actually the best day to have the job.

First on his schedule was class time with the ten-year-olds. This brought a smile to his face. For just as today was Lincoln's eightieth birthday, everyone else on board was having a birthday too. The Lustrum Celebration was a special day for the children in particular though. A new generation was born every five years, so the Lustrum (half-decade) birthdays were as joyful occasions as they were sad ones—probably more joyful, if you took an honest poll of the Ship. 8 new babies were going to be delivered starting early in the afternoon. Another first, today the five-year-olds would be given direct access to the Ship through their implants. *Plugging-in* was a gradual process, but their first experiences with eye and ear enhancement would take place today. The ten-year-olds were set to begin work on the farms that afternoon, actually picking some of the food they'd all eat later at the great feast. This tenure on the farm began a five year spell of work for them, though many people choose to pursue at least some of this work throughout the course of the rest of their lives. Helping to grow, tend to, and harvest the food was the one and only job required of every single person on the Ship.

Today was a crucial day for the three youngest generations, all excited to be passing into distinct new phases of their lives. Especially important was the youngest, however. The ocular manipulation lessons that would take place in the five-year-olds' classroom were fun learning programs made up of little games that progressively got more difficult, gradually introducing new features and utilities that the children could unlock and explore. Today's lesson included an interactive demo that Lincoln still remembered vividly for the simple reason that it had blown his young mind. He was glad that he'd be there for that.

Plugging-in was easy. Every person on the Ship carried in their bodies four advanced systems, all micro-implanted. The main operating piece in the brain coordinated control of the other three. This system was implanted in a quick surgery on the day of birth: nothing more than a series of non-intrusive injections which micro-robotically assembled into a highly connected neural-microprocessor that developed along with the developing brain. At age one came footpad implants, which were a system of magnetized pads allowing for traction on the surfaces of the Ship. The last two remaining surgeries had been performed on the five-year-olds early that morning. They didn't hurt much—certainly far less traumatic than many of the other things people used to do to their kids—but the surgeries were normalized so that the children actually looked forward to them, as a rite of passage. Matching audio implants were inserted into the inner ears in a simple surgery, then eye implants were introduced via a liquid eye drop solution, beginning to assemble immediately. This made the eyes burn for a few hours, but it was certainly worth it, well, pretty much instantly. Once in place, slight eye movements could manipulate multiple independent screens in each eye. This allowed you to communicate directly with the Ship, accessing innumerable programs and experiencing a mind-numbingly vast compendium of information, superimposed over your field of view and directly piped into your ears. Or, if you wanted, you could play the media of your choice on the walls, or on the ceiling, or the floor, in many combinations of audio and visual.

Through these implants the five-year-olds would be gaining personal access to the Ship. Information is the ultimate source of power, after all, and today the youngsters were being plugged into the most advanced sentient supercomputer ever known to have existed in the Galaxy. This direct link with the Ship served so many functions and roles that its importance could not be reasonably articulated to the non-connected. *Plugging-in* facilitated several types of communications, including real-time messaging with others and the Ship. Education as well as research was conducted through this interface; from quick searches for information, to school projects on specific topics, to long-term, oftentimes life-long queries on such far-ranging subjects as temporal physics, human psychology, death and dying, experimental exobiology, or comparative Earth history. The Ship contained every art form ever imagined so far by the human race. This made the eye-ear-brain interface the principal source of entertainment on the Ship, providing instant, front-row-seat admission to anything ever put into tangible form: every written work, every movie, every game, every melody and every performance ever captured by a recording device on Earth at the time of the Ship's departure, plus many more iterations of every category added since then, all instantly accessible. People uploaded their life's work into the Ship (including many discoveries far beyond anything ever comprehended on Earth), and once you had a connection you had access to it all. Today was a life changing event, for the young ones were becoming connected to everything known in their world and to everyone else in it.

Of course, access was kept extremely low at first. A basic tenet was no screens of any kind, if avoidable, before the age of four. [Sadly, history shows us that people literally scrambled their children's brains with heavy exposure to screens at young ages.] Developing primate brains are wired to interact with others in a real environment, learning the enormous range of human behaviors from copying the people they love and trust, not staring mindlessly at images on a wall in an alpha-brain-wave haze. Thus, on the Ship, up until the age of four, the children only interacted with other people.

Still naked, Lincoln popped his head into the corridor outside of his room. Clean clothes were typically delivered and stored while you were out, but his late start had caused his clothing order to be locked out. Thankfully, a pile of fabric was folded neatly on the floor right next to his door. Looking both ways to make sure no one was coming, he snatched the pile. The door quickly swooshed closed behind him.

With a command issued through very precise movements within his left eye, Lincoln turned the long wall beside the bed into a mirror. He picked up the clothes, examining them closely before he put them on. The pants were basic enough: navy blue with a single wide, bright silver pinstripe running down the

outside of each leg. In the formal style, the pants totally enclosed each leg, covering his normally bare feet with the silken material. The *Captain's Red* shirt was fancier; sporting perfect lines, with tasteful gold accoutrements and high V-neck collar trimmed in the same silver as the pants. The outfit, Lincoln's last-ever clothing request, had been settled on two days prior—with Helen's seal of approval of course. It fit exceptionally well.

Captain Lincoln certainly still looked the part.

Suddenly an internal alarm designed to be ever so uncomfortable buzzed in his ears while bold text flashed across both eyes. It was abrasive, meant to be annoying as all hell.

"Shit," said Lincoln with a shake of the head.

He finished with a quick mouth-foam shot pulled

from another narrow tube in the hygiene station, swishing it around a few times while he shaped his dark hair into place with his hands. When he was done he spat the mix back into the same tube, then took a siphon from the water tube to rinse. He needed to hurry. Even at a decent pace the classrooms were far from there, with lots of people to maneuver through as they all prepared for the day's events.

Queasy, Lincoln's stomach gurgled, a tangle of knots once more.

With a command issued by just a twitch of an eye, Lincoln toggled the music feed from external to personal as he left his room. Walking the hallways quickly, the *Stones* now blasted privately in his ears.

THREE

After your death you will be
what you were before your birth.

Arthur Schopenhauer
Deceased 21 September 1860 AD (aged 72)
Frankfurt, German Confederation, Earth

The ever-changing internal configurations of the *Hope Eternal* would be impossible to navigate without some sort of guidance from the Ship. For deep inside, no hallway was ever the same. The rearrangements usually occurred approximately on the hour, and mostly in the various blocks of space where people weren't already congregated. Not only did the hallways change, but even the doorways leading into and out of the rooms moved to different positions. During the day the small cells near the core where people slept were folded back into the Ship (the empty space no longer needed), freeing up room for enhanced recreation, all sorts of different gatherings, music and art studios, and more.

The polar opposite, the Classrooms were permanent bastions close to the outer hull, nestled between two large tracts of farms where the artificial gravity was the highest. With all of the congestion in the halls (mostly people getting ready for the party), it took Lincoln a while to get to his destination.

The Teachers Haxley and Gorwell both glanced up as the door in back of Classroom 2 slid open and Lincoln quietly strode in. The two men sat at the front of the large, circular room, sharing the long black Teacher's console. It was a bright space with a very high ceiling. 8 deskstations fanned out facing the Teachers, each with a child sitting comfortably at it. The kids were totally engrossed in something flashing on the screens in front of them. There were also other seats around the perimeter of the large room, a few of them occupied with adults, whom Lincoln acknowledged with a nod. Not wanting to interrupt, he sat at the nearest empty seat on the perimeter.

The ping of a private message rang in Lincoln's ears the moment he sat down. He opened the communication in a screen in his eye.

Haxley: *Captain Lincoln, we should be done with this very soon… maybe a matter of 10 minutes or so.*

There's a logical break coming up which should segue into your talk quite well, I think.

Haxley: *Please, just a few more minutes?*

Lincoln's response was effortless, precise movements in his eyes honed from a lifetime of use allowing him to type out the words almost as quick as he thought of them.

Lincoln: *Of course, Hax. Take all the time you need! I could use some time to gather my thoughts anyway. Also, I may not get to this, but I thought it was fitting. If I don't, can you please start what would've been my next scheduled lecture with it?*

Lincoln: *It's here: <u>Lincoln/Lecture Notes/R.I.P./A Psalm of Life.</u>*

Haxley: *Ah—the Longfellow. That's a good choice. I'll make sure that they see it.*

Lincoln: *Thanks, as always, my friend.*

After a few quiet minutes the children simultaneously looked up at their teachers, whatever media they were watching finished. Their deskstations were now black.

Haxley broke the silence of the room.

"So as we can see, it's quite clear that human health took a severe downward turn after the first advent of agriculture. That seems a bit of a paradox at first, doesn't it? Yet Earth's fossil record was very clear: Stone Age populations were taller and significantly healthier than the people who came after them. Indeed, in every instance of initial large scale agricultural production in history, the peoples' diet *devolves*, going from nutritional richness and variety to the reliance on just a few types of grain (typically wheat, maize, or rice), and maybe supplementing with some meat and dairy if they could. And we have just seen some of the results of this: significantly smaller body sizes in these populations, much shorter life spans, and a spike in all sorts of deadly diseases. In fact, we have very detailed records of many of the plagues that killed off huge percentages of ancient peoples, all of them arising out of cities densely packed with people, livestock, and vermin, all living in close contact because of how their social and industrial environments had evolved."

Haxley rapidly touched the screen in front of him, looking for something in particular. Quickly finding the folder he wanted, he transferred a ream of pertinent information onto the screens of the room and hence into the children's schoolwork folder. Their screens flashed with graphs and charts showing the various plagues that had ravaged human societies throughout the ages.

"Combined together, these facts help underscore the notion that the origin of farming is a defining event in human history because of the way that it fundamentally changes societies. As we have been learning, traditional hunter and gatherer societies were small, cohesive tribes of people. This was the way of life for *Homo Sapiens* for 90% of their existence on the planet! Think about it. There was little or no privacy to speak of in a small tribe. Food was generally divided and distributed equally. The ideas of working together, group welfare, group identity, mutual trust and dependence were the rule. And since food was relatively abundant, and there was nothing really stopping others from leaving your group—there was no way to control other people. Leaders were followed because they *earned* the respect of their tribe, through knowledge and wisdom, not because they were bigger and stronger—or richer. In many ways, our society has evolved *back* to this sort of life."

"But once large scale agriculture enters the picture and regional populations reach critical mass—and we see this in the rise of major civilization after major civilization—the inevitable happens. Everything changes from what was before: the nature of power and status; social structures, including and especially the expression of sexuality; overall quality of life for the average person; even the nature of worship to the Gods … THESE ALL CHANGE. Food that had been gathered or hunted now had to be planted, tended, harvested, stored, traded, AND defended, so, for the first times in history, fences and walls were put up. And since land could now be owned, possessed, and passed down from generation to generation, for the first time in history paternity becomes a crucial concern. Indeed, this may be where the idea of monogamy first really took hold—blood lines needed to be protected to ensure claims to the precious land. Consequently, this moves women from a critical, central, respected role in the foraging, hunter-gatherer society to just another possession that a man could earn—another thing to defend along with his livestock and his land. The human impulse for sharing, something that had evolved in us for millennia—an irrefutable instinct of a social animal, and especially a primate—is put aside. Interdependence switches to independence; responsibility to the group switches to standing on your own two feet."

Haxley put the words on the walls and screens of the room as he spoke them.

> *Thou shalt not covet they*
> *neighbor's house, thou shalt not*
> *covet thy neighbor's wife, nor his*
> *manservant, nor his maidservant,*
> *nor his ox, nor his ass, nor*
> *anything that is thy neighbor's.*

"That's the bible, laying the groundwork for property law. To be clear, laws aren't a bad thing—by any means. Institutionalization is the problem: the laws that inevitably grow up around power. An inflexible status quo that is soon made unquestionable purely because of the weight of its own power."

Haxley paused, making sure that he still had the attention of the class before continuing.

"Every war that has ever been fought has really been about other people's things: specifically land and the resources on or in that land. The need for more— more food, more women, more slaves, more gold, more room, more oil, or more water—usually ends in a very bad way for a whole lot of innocent people. You see, it's very easy to go back to the tribal instinct of our ancestors. The human brain seems to have evolved to emotionally commit to only a small slice of geography and a limited band of kin—your tribe of people—and only look two or three generations into the future, if that. This Paleolithic hard-wiring makes sense in many ways. Looking too far ahead or too far away doesn't make much sense from a Darwinian standpoint, does it? Especially with cave lions and all sorts of other things trying to eat you! Life was short and hard compared to how we have it. A premium was placed on close attention to the near future: survival, food and shelter, reproducing from an early age, and not much else … which in itself explains a lot in terms of basic human behaviors. This hard-wired, inherent short-sightedness—ignoring distant possibilities—combined with very aggressive tribalism, is a terrible combination of traits that have absolutely marauded through every chapter of human history. The violence that often comes from it traces its roots from the dawn of recorded history, straight up through modern Earth up until the day that we left it."

Haxley paused, looking around at the beautiful children.

"The question I pose to all of you is this. The benefits of agriculture, especially to us, could not be more clear: our lives depend on the food that we grow with our own hands. But when you look at Earth as we left it, with a human species at its pinnacle in terms of geographic settlement, technological power and productivity, it's quite clear that many of the ideas that had taken root in that society were clearly only by-products of doing things the old, easy way—and, in plain fact, a path which was driving the planet in the wrong direction for most of the life left on it."

Haxley paused once more, his question now ripe.

"Our little tribe knows better now, but how do we make sure that a society first beginning to live and grow on a new planet will hold onto and act with this wisdom?"

A boy was the first to cautiously raise his hand.

"We are different, father," he began.

The other teacher, Gorwell, raised an eyebrow while he put his left hand to his chin, stroking his small beard. It was a bit of a trademark of sorts.

"We are extremely lucky compared to the people who came before us," the boy continued, his confidence growing with each word. "Evolution is the process of improvement … We are nearing a perfect situation, able to use our technology to fundamentally alter what we eat, our environment—even ourselves. It would be highly unlikely that we would go backwards from here, given all that we know today, and how we've evolved."

Gorwell continued to thoughtfully finger the dark hair on his chin as he spoke. "My son, human history is absolutely filled with people who thought exactly the same way as you. Sure … It certainly feels like we've finally triumphed against this incomprehensibly bloody and terrible past, against very long odds indeed. But I believe that it's an error to conclude that *here and now* is so obviously better than *there and then.*"

With a smile, music began to play out of the walls of the room and very soon Gorwell began to sing. Their Teacher's voice was true; a jazzy tenor evocative of Sinatra, with just the touch of vibrato on the long notes.

Blue skies
Smiling at me
Nothing but blue skies
Do I see

Bluebirds
Singing a song
Nothing but bluebirds
All day long

Haxley touched the console in front of them as his partner continued to sing. Suddenly, not only the deskscreens but all of the wall space of the circular room began to flash with grainy movies of the people of the time. The videos were of the United States of America in the late 1920's, in hauntingly choppy black and white.

Never saw the sun shining so bright
Never saw things going so right
Noticing the days hurrying by
When you're in love, my how they fly

Blue days
All of them gone
Nothing but blue skies
From now on

I never saw the sun shining so bright
Never saw things going so right
Noticing the days hurrying by
When you're in love, my how they fly

Blue days
All of them gone
Nothing but blue skies
From now on

"Beautiful song, isn't it?" said Gorwell when he finished. "Fantastic melody. *Blue Skies*[3] was THE most popular song in a nation that was thriving, full of wonder and ingenuity and promise. Yet, only a few years later the country—and a considerable amount of the rest of the world along with it—plunged into a depression that starved many thousands, ultimately culminating in a great war that killed millions, in a confrontation of countless atrocities. It was death beyond comprehension."

Gorwell made sure to make eye contact with each child as he spoke.

"It's a deeply comforting thought to think that we're the lucky ones, past an age like that. It actually goes directly to the innate tribalism that Teacher Haxley just discussed. That idea, that *we are the best, the blessed, the chosen ones so lucky to be alive,* is all too common across time and history. It is not an answer to anything! Ours is a random moment in eternity—a tiny thread of precious time among uncountable moments, across an incomprehensible large Galaxy."

Focusing back on the boy who'd first spoken, he continued.

"It is also a common mistake to conclude that evolution can or will ever end. And societies, just like organisms, adapt over generations to changing conditions. Any gained modifications can be beneficial, but they are not really *improvements* because external conditions never stop shifting. Here, on the Ship, we don't feel any change at all. We're basically sealed in a cave, after all. We've mastered the atom and genetics and simplified our lives to great effect—and we're happy as clams about it all. But that doesn't mean that change isn't happening! We're just incapable of noticing it. Who knows, though? Sometimes change is very sudden. What if, totally unbeknownst to us, there's a small asteroid zooming through space less than a light-day away and approaching fast? We certainly can't move in time so we'd be destroyed—no longer the amazing, stunning genius of a species that we think we are."

Gorwell smiled at the child, putting it as gently as possible.

"Even though you can't see it, my son, things are

changing. Things *always* change, given enough time and pressure. The very thought of that is scary to some, but change is absolutely nothing to be afraid of. It is a simple fact of life."

Working seamlessly with his partner, Haxley sent another media packet to the deskscreens. He opened a subfolder and soon a rotating parade of images began to populate the walls of the room. They were all very strange organisms: giant, hairy beasts, some with great teeth and claws, other goliaths with tusks or great horns growing out of their skulls.

"History," said Haxley, "shows us that when entering a new environment, humans inevitably eat their way right down the food chain. First to go among animal species are always the big and the slow. As a general rule all around Planet Earth, whenever and wherever humans entered a virgin environment most of the megafauna quickly vanished. Also doomed were most of the easily captured ground birds, tortoises, reptiles, insects and so on. Usually only smaller and swifter species are able to hang on, and only in much smaller numbers."

The walls now flashed with all manner of long-gone birds and reptiles, soon followed with a rainbow of colorful sea life, also long extinct.

"It would certainly seem *logical* to think that a species lives in balance with other plants and animals in its natural environment, but human beings are a prime example of what you call a switching predator. On Earth we ate pretty much everything we could get our hands on: from snails and crickets to lobsters, octopi, fish, even whales, turkeys, rabbits to woolly mammoths … not to mention seaweed, carrots, mushrooms, rice, apples, and potatoes. Humans, as another general rule, tend to overharvest most animal species to the point of extinction, then just switch to something else. The human tendency for expediency—going the easy route when it comes to basic resources—trends out in many directions from there."

With a touch of his finger all of the screens went black.

A girl raised her hand next. She was one of the smallest of the children but she spoke firmly, with a confidence well beyond her young age.

"But father, when we finally get there it *will* be different. We have the ability to seed the world responsibly. By design, we have no parentage—and I don't see that changing. Therefore, by design, we are a controlled population. Our society is very different because of this, plus the technology that we possess. It *is* possible for a different beginning, a new start. We must never lose hope."

"Fine." Gorwell conceded the point with a curt nod of his head. "Let's say that we do manage to retain all of our great knowledge of history and science, and continue to act with wisdom when we finally arrive at *Earth 2.0*. Still, we need to remember what I just said about evolution: <u>external conditions always dictate</u>. An untouched, virgin planet will be a radically different environment than a closed-system starship … and that reality will immediately change everything—no matter what you think. Abundance is easy, and we will probably spread out. According to pretty much all of human history that may well bring disaster: the possibility of a mass genocide of unique, never-studied, flora and fauna, planet-wide."

"The question still remains …" Haxley jumped in, continuing the thought. "Our little tribe knows better now, in *this* particular time and place. But how do we make sure that a society living on a brand new world will be able to hold on to all of our critical knowledge? How do we ensure that our people will continue to act with all of the great wisdom that we have acquired?"

Haxley pinged Lincoln.

Haxley: *How's that for a set up?*

Lincoln: *You're good, brother.*

Lincoln raised his hand as he loudly cleared his throat. The children whirled around in their seats, surprise turning into delight.

"It's all very easy, actually," said Lincoln with a wide smile. "The answer is the golden rule … love. Love and respect the people around you, just as you love and respect yourself. Teach your children this love by your words, but especially through your deeds; through all of the examples of your life. Because wisdom should be passed down with love, and with the trust that comes with love. With loving trust is the very best way for anything to be passed down."

Lincoln smiled broadly as he stood to his impressive height and adjusted his crisp scarlet shirt. Then he strode confidently to the front of the class.

FOUR

Why is it that we rejoice at a birth
and grieve at a funeral?
It is because we are not the person
involved.

Mark Twain
Deceased 21 April 1910 AD (aged 74)
Redding, United States of America, Earth

"Welcome, Captain Lincoln," said Haxley as he and Gorwell stood up from the Teacher's console. Haxley gestured to the instructor's bench as the two men moved to empty seats in the back.

Lincoln decided to sit. It was good to be eye-to-eye with kids.

"Happy birthday, everybody," he said earnestly after a moment, nervous for the first time that he could remember.

"Today is a big day. I remember when I was ten. Being able to pick food for the Ship for the first time, trading your time and energy to feed and nourish others … there's something very special about that. Some would say spiritual. There's a reason why some people never leave their jobs on the farms. Tending and picking food is our only real duty here. It's a duty to others, and that makes you feel good about yourself. Starting today you will begin to learn many new things: production cycles, botany and genetics, new smells and tastes, but also a sense of duty to others, the essentials of making and following through with a plan and the gratification of working with your hands, among many other things."

Lincoln paused, searching for the right words. Perspective was important here. He was once like them. He remembered how exciting life was for them at this moment—it was a great blur of a time. Even today, a day of deep emotions for so many, the kids were mostly immune. They probably wouldn't feel much emotion at all, besides excitement. Maybe they'd be sad in a few days, after it really sunk in that Lincoln and his brothers and sisters were gone for good. It would fade quickly, though; a shallow grief without the depth of wisdom and experience.

Lincoln looked at the boy seated in the exact desk-station he'd sat at when he was ten, the far-right seat in the back row, imagining old Captain Whitman speaking to him just as he was speaking to the boy today. To recognize the moment was surreal.

"Today is even bigger than food cycles, though," he began again, "as important as that is. Today is my last day with you, and that makes me extremely sad. I've known all of you since you were babies and I love each of you dearly."

Lincoln made eye contact with each of them, nodding his head as he spoke. "Today, the last day of my life, there's nothing more I'd like to do than to be your teacher once more. And today's topic is a particularly gruesome one: death, specifically your own."

The Captain let his words resonate, now in full control of his well-honed speech-making skills. It was breathlessly silent in the high-ceilinged room. Like an old cathedral the power came from the altar in the front, the rest of the people there all afraid to speak. Right now the only life seemed to be coming from the deep voice at the front of the room.

"Death is not an easy topic," Lincoln said. "I've been thinking about it a lot myself—too much, I know that now. I've read pretty much everything I could get my hands on regarding dying, and spent many a sleepless night pondering it all. It took a very long time for me to make any sense of it ... to be at peace with my own death, at least as best I could. But I still can't say that my entire brain has fully accepted it. I couldn't sleep again last night, for I don't even know how many nights in a row."

Lincoln looked around at them seriously.

"The bad news is that it never gets easy. Dealing with death only gets harder as you get older, especially as you get closer to it."

Lincoln decided to stand—a spontaneous gesture. The uneasy feeling kicking around in the pit of his stomach had come back, *impending doom mode* flicked on again in the back of his brain. He moved around the Teacher's console and leaned against the front of it, crossing his arms over his gurgling stomach.

"My first thoughts concerning my own impending demise came suddenly. I remember it very specifically, in fact. I was with Captain Kennedy when he'd mentioned that we'd already begun making preparations for the harvest for tonight's feast. It hit me suddenly, right then and there. I only had six months left! After that it became really hard to concentrate on anything else … It was like my life was already over. I couldn't sleep anymore, which made me feel really tired all of the time, creating a very bad cycle."

"So, I did what I needed to do. I did what we're all taught to do. I started to look for answers. Of course, to find an answer you need the right question. My most immediate question was: why was I feeling the way that I was—extremely depressed? But the answer was so easy. The end of your life is the end of you. I don't want to die … even now, knowing that I must. Even after mostly accepting it, with meditation and plenty of rationalization, the worst part is the unconscious, animal part of my brain. This part of me has been fighting it the whole way, the whole time."

It still was. Lincoln felt that initial sensation of needing to vomit. His bone-dry mouth suddenly filled with saliva, his stomach raging up a storm. He took a slow, deep, controlling breath, then another.

"My next questions involved how to make these feelings go away … how to somehow accept my sorry state of affairs and get on living the little life I had left. Well, I'm sorry to report that I still don't have a great answer on how to do that, either, even after months of studying and all those sleepless nights."

Lincoln sighed, looking up at the ceiling as he thought of what to say next. The dome high overhead displayed a mostly cloudless blue summer sky. The warmth of the light streaming down from the small yellow sun felt good on his skin and he basked in it for a moment, facing up to it with his eyes closed for another few breaths.

"Captain Lincoln?" a child asked, finally breaking the silence. Lincoln opened his eyes and saw that it was the boy seated in his old chair.

"Captain Adam discusses the religions of Earth a lot in his later journals. Did you find that they helped you?"

Lincoln smiled, mostly at the boldness of the boy.

"Yes. Religion is a very natural place to start. Even when humans didn't know much of anything we still tried our best to explain our world. All of the world's religions started there, in the same place: explanation. They were all trying to explain how things worked. In the very first religions the sun was a god and the Earth a goddess—both viewpoints basically more correct than not, depending on how you look at it. The ancient peoples made up all sorts of fantastic myths to explain the existence of the moon and the stars, plants and animals and the rest of the natural world. They made up stories to explain where all the different languages came from, and why people looked differently. The Greek, Egyptian, and Mayan cultures, for example, while on one hand correctly describing scientific explanations for many phenomena, still clung to the gods as the supernatural agents when they couldn't explain the rest: the working of the sunset and the tides, the randomness of the weather and the wind. This history is very interesting, and often times very poignant, but, truth be told, I didn't find much worth there. We know too much about the Universe now, so none of the stories make much sense."

"Still, and as Captain Adam discusses at length, religion is very intriguing as both a concept and development. *Billions* of people in the highly advanced civilization of Earth were religious believers when we left them—despite all that we knew about the Universe then! And studies showed that these religious people had less difficulty concentrating than non-believers. They were less nervous, less anxious and tense, and had less difficulty falling asleep—totally nailing my symptoms! Religion seemed to have a remarkable way of providing comfort, and that's exactly what I needed."

Lincoln shook his head slowly, staring deeply into the black floor.

"But that's precisely where I hit a wall. This man Sigmund Freud said that the faithful clung to God's existence in the absence of evidence because the alternative—an empty void—is so much worse.[4] It's crystal clear. Religions are very elaborate mechanisms for denial. Almost across the board, the comfort that the religious found came from simply denying death's reality. Comfort came from creating an afterlife ... a fantastical place where the soul goes after the physical body is gone, when the mind, which is contained within a brain, is the place where consciousness comes from. That doesn't make any sense! But, if you follow God's will this soul of yours will float away to a heaven of infinite worldly delights, filled with only the right religion of good people—your tribe only—until the end of eternity. Or, maybe it's a karmic recycling of the soul back into the Earth, or into nature, or as a spirit destined to protect your descendants. It's all the same though. Redemption and salvation. Martyrdom. Angels living in the clouds or walking among us. Immortality. They're all places where your mind can find some semblance of comfort in; havens during the worst storms of your life. A switch that you can throw in your brain so you don't have to think about the tough stuff. It's all about escape, places where the mind can go to hide from the fear because the alternative—nothing at all—is much worse."

Lincoln shrugged, shaking his head.

"So there's the catch—and it's an immense one. According to most religions, in order to not fear death you're instructed from childhood on to believe in fairy tales that don't survive logic and science and, thus, the reality of other people around you. In order to have peace of mind you need to relinquish the critical facilities of your mind … or never have had a chance at a free, thinking mind in the first place! Bury your head deep enough in the sand and it doesn't matter what's coming. You can't see it. You don't care."

Lincoln looked up at the sky for a moment. Overriding the setting with his eyes, he turned the ceiling into a stunning starscape of the Milky Way—one of his very favorites. As the light in the room dimmed, he compensated by making the stars shine much brighter than normal. Waves of radiation rippled among several of the great constellations.

"Religion certainly took me down some interesting hallways, though. It was fascinating to examine how all of the various religious institutions changed over time; building up slowly at first but always trying to reconcile themselves with their societies at large as they grew; trying to survive and thrive despite the ever-increasing sphere of understanding about the laws of science. It's inevitable, essentially a rule: a good way of organizing people becomes obedience to the inevitable hierarchy it creates. Institutions made of men become corrupted by vanity and greed, always trying to build on their already vaunted power and place in their respective societies. Then, in the worst manifestation—which Teacher Haxley talked about before—leaders used religion to justify war; ignoring the beautiful words of Jesus and Mohammed on how to treat other people ... with love and respect; twisting and warping, if not completely ignoring the great wisdom of peace to hypocritically commit atrocities against others because they're a different tribe. This occurs over and over again in history. The people of Earth never learned that lesson."

Lincoln looked up again, slowly this time, intending to draw other eyes up with him. In a few seconds he caused a big star over the center of the room to go supernova. The star burst with a flash of light before becoming a beautiful fluorescent halo of gas and dust.

"There weren't many answers for me in religion, but it wasn't entirely fruitless. Christianity is based on the self-sacrifice of a man. That idea totally resonates with my personal situation—dying so that others can live. It's almost exactly like me, and it comes down to love at the heart of it all. I also found it interesting how so many great people were stuck in a society where one ideology was their only possible reality, yet they managed to create works that still resonate thousands of years later. Take the composer Mozart. This man dies on Earth at the age of thirty-five while writing a requiem mass—a symphony intended for the Christian funeral after death. Feeling sick, he even tells his friends, *I fear I am writing a requiem for myself!*' Somehow, Mozart creates this symphony with timbres and melodies which totally capture the immense heaviness of death. Through his music, Mozart is expressing many of the same feelings that I was still struggling with myself."

Lincoln toggled on music through the walls around them, pumping up the bass a bit more for good measure:

After a while Lincoln lowered the plaintive music.

"One thing that helps when thinking about life and death is to look at a birth and a death as two sides of the same coin. That may sound odd at first, but hear me out. It's easy to see the miracle of life in the birth of another person. The miracle is celebrated, an easy joy, but no one really thinks deeply about it because we simply don't have to. We are literally programmed to love them. Yet consciousness takes time to creep in and take hold in a person. It takes a while until the birth is really appreciated for what life truly is … the birth of a new baby is the celebration of a unique, special creature with a mind and body of its own, completely full of promise."

"Now, let's flip that coin. When someone dies the

miracle of birth is perfectly clear, instantly on full display. Because it's easy to see how special a person was when they're gone. Unlike here, on Earth people would often die very suddenly. A shock—a paralyzing, devastating grief would take hold as family and friends were immediately forced to recognize that a unique, cherished, idiosyncratic individual who meant so much to them was now gone forever. In that sense we have it much easier here: a guaranteed eighty years, with healthy bodies and minds, no illness, plus a tranquil life with plenty of other people and things to keep us occupied. Pretty much any person ever born in the history of Earth would take our deal, no questions asked. Yet here, on this Ship with this deal in hand, knowing exactly when death is coming is still a very hard thing to accept. It's natural to hurt, to grieve. It's natural to mourn—others, and even yourself."

Lincoln took another deep breath.

"Perspective is also very important. Another thing that has really helped me is to try to think about the big picture. It helps if you can appreciate the miracle that is our lives, yours and mine, but being able to see the big picture takes an imagination that some people never really find. Appreciate that the odds of *us being us* were so astronomically small. Every single molecule currently inside our bodies was flung into existence from the death of some star unfathomably long ago. For example, do you know where the water we drink originally came from … besides it being our own pee? It's actually not from Earth at all! All our water was harvested on the Moon, after purposefully crashing thousands of asteroids and meteorites on its surface to release all of it. All of these molecules, inside your bodies right now, are billions and billions of years old—far older than we can really conceptualize with our brains. This …," he tapped his chest, "our corporal form of star dust and energy, has integrated into a body and formed a mind from a singular original cell, and that single cell came into existence out of a veritable maze of infinite possible outcomes! The genes making up the recipes used by your cells survived and adapted through countless ancestors of an untold number of species until finally, miraculously, YOU have emerged, in this particular time and place, sitting in front of me right now and processing these very words."

"The plain fact of the matter is that every single one of us is incredibly lucky just to be alive. Yet to some, especially in the past, the immense randomness of our great luck was too difficult to fathom … so they automatically tried to stamp it with some sort of divine blueprint which made them feel better. Like I said, it's actually a lack of imagination that does this."

Lincoln paused for a moment, making sure that

they understood what he was trying to explain.

"It helps to truly appreciate how astronomical the odds were that YOU, the individual, conscious, thinking mind that is processing these words—and belongs only to you—came into existence. Our own lives are the one given throughout each of our existences, yet so many countless other lives contributed to us being here, where we find ourselves now. It's not just all of our direct human ancestors either, but the organisms before them, before our ancestors were even furry little mammals, before we could even live out of the water. Little pieces of all of these ancestors managed to survive and some of the pieces still live within us now. Out of this crazy chaos of the Universe we were born and then we are shaped, by all of the things that we see and do and especially by the people who've loved us the most. You, me, all of us—we've all hit on one tremendous jackpot. Appreciate that. Do not squander it."

Pushing himself up off the console, Lincoln moved back to the bench and sat down tiredly. Letting his guard down, suddenly the full range of emotions played across his face. The Captain's dark eyes carried the full force of truth.

"When it's your own death that you're struggling with though? I'm sorry to report that there are no tricks, kiddos. Grab on to whatever you can and hold on for a very bumpy ride. The big picture view helps, and I strongly suggest grabbing the people you love close as soon as it's possible. But understand that it's not easy, any way you cut it. Everything comes to an end, you included, whether you decide to face this fact or not."

Lincoln ended with a tight, somewhat forced smile, his hands clasped together on top of the console. It was not entirely what he'd intended to say, but it was good enough.

"So, that's my speech," he said as he leaned back. "I really hope it helps you when you need it . . . if you need it."

After a few seconds of deep silence, Haxley spoke from his seat at the back of the room. "Thank you, Captain Lincoln. You words are very wise. You are a good man and a great friend and you will be missed by many."

Lincoln forced an even wider smile, even though the words made him incredibly sad. Yet his eyes couldn't cover the lie that his mouth was trying to sell.

"I think it's a good time to open the floor now," said Gorwell. "Are there any questions, children?"

The bold boy in Lincoln's old chair immediately raised his hand.

"Captain, can you please send us your personal files?"

"Of course," Lincoln replied with a smile. It was a sincere request, but the child could have easily found the files himself with just a little bit of work. Still, Lincoln couldn't deny the fact that the request made him happy. The boy was very much like he was: serious, hard-working, with a powerful competitive streak, and always looking for a better way to do things. And even in the bad ways too, sometimes stubborn and impatient, occasionally bordering on impetuous. Lincoln had struggled with a very similar mix himself. It wasn't always an easy combination to deal with, but eventually the child could become a good leader—if he chose to be. To do so the boy would need to bring integrity to that competitive drive, wield penetration and prudence, not the selfish me-first attitude that he still sometimes clung to.

Lincoln sent the folder of his collected works to each of the children, including a quick cover note personalized to each of them. He put his very last entries—a sort of life summary—on top, some of it linked to Captain Adam's last works, then dumped everything else into various subfolders below. The files included everything Lincoln had ever generated onboard the Ship: ten years of official Captain's logs and schedules, his doctoral work in gravitational turbulence, various other journal entries, plus bookmarks to favorite music, literature, games, movies, and more.

A girl raised a hand next, curiosity plastered all over her face. "Thank you, Captain Lincoln," she said sincerely. "We all love you very much. If you had the chance to experience one thing on Earth, what would it be?"

Lincoln smiled warmly. She was one of the dreamers of her generation. This was a common game with a universe of answers. The question had to do with access, really: despite living in what was essentially a windowless cave hurtling through space at mind-melting speed, the people of the Ship still felt extremely connected to the Earth through all the things its people had left them; all of their pictures and movies, words and faces and songs.

Lincoln turned on his Captain affectation again. He spoke slower, in a deeper, more resonant voice.

"An Earthling named Henry Beston wrote: 'The three great elemental sounds in nature are the sound of rain, the sound of wind in a primeval wood, and the sound of the outer ocean on a beach. I have heard them all, and of the three elemental voices, that of ocean is the most awesome, beautiful and varied.[5]' I would want something like that—a good, strong dose of nature. Maybe old Beston's beach on Cape Cod, on the Atlantic."

A long section of one of the walls suddenly turned into a large sun hovering just over the horizon of a calm ocean. Taking full control of the scene on the wall, Lincoln narrated as he continued to build it.

"Watch the sun set slowly over the ocean … then watch as the stars begin to come out, twinkling into existence one by one. Then, slowly, the moon comes up … Then feel the power of a great storm front moving in off the coast."

A storm began, suddenly darkening the wall even further. A rush of cold air blew in from the ocean, the wind howling until it stopped abruptly. Then the image changed.

"Or, maybe I should chose to look up at great, snow-capped mountains."

Now the wall of the room turned into a continuous, 360 degree screen. It looked as if they were in a valley, surrounded on all sides by dark, jagged peaks capped in white. The room rapidly grew much colder too.

"There's something about the great power and majesty of nature that seems very good for centering a soul … for helping puny beings like us put things into perspective."

Lincoln smiled wryly, that Hollywood grin again.

"But a single answer is boring! We could see the Grand Canyon. Or Earth from orbit. Or an elementary school of children exactly your age. An ant hill or an elephant! You should poll the Ship, my dear—I wonder if anyone has actually done that before. I'm sure you'd get some really fabulous answers."

Smiling happily, the girl seemed to be already half-lost in a daydream.

Another boy raised his hand.

"Captain Lincoln, do you have any regrets in life?"

Lincoln shook his head no.

"To me, regret just doesn't feel right—as a feeling. I've had a great life with no complaints. I have a woman who loves me and many dear friends. There are certainly times in my life where I should have reacted differently, responded better to a person or situation, or made a better choice. But, *c'est la vie*—that is life. Life is one big classroom. You react the best you can in the moment, and hopefully you've learned your lessons when you catch yourself looking back with—"

For the second time that day, suddenly Lincoln's ears rang with that jarring buzz, the alarm blinking large text in front of his eyes:

"Damn!" said Lincoln with a shake of the head. "Sorry, guys. That was my alarm. I'm sorry to say that I'm almost out of time here. It's becoming a very sad theme to my day."

Lincoln finished with a tight smile as he stood.

"Not having enough time with you guys right now is the one thing I certainly do regret."

With that, the old captain began to slowly work his way around the room, saying farewell to each child, individual by individual. Every parting was personalized, not only by name and affection, but with Lincoln doling out all sorts of compliments, encouragements, and general pieces of fatherly advice. The goodbyes were liberally dosed with handshakes and hair-ruffling and a whole lot of hugs.

After some time, and 8 happy customers later, Lincoln was finished. He looked around the room one last time as he stood near the door, a content smile spread across his still-handsome face.

"I will see you guys later, okay?"

With that, Lincoln turned and left them, once again entering the hallways in a hurry to get somewhere else.

* * *

When Lincoln was gone Haxley sent something to the deskscreens of the Classroom. The text appears on the next page. Class discussion continued, first revolving around the poem, then Lincoln's lecture, and finally the children's perception of the Captain himself.

Lincoln was also wrong about one thing: they all missed him immediately.

A Psalm of Life

*Tell me not, in mournful
numbers,
Life is but an empty dream!
For the soul is dead that
slumbers,
And things are not what they
seem.*

*Life is real! Life is earnest!
And the grave is not its goal;
Dust thou art, to dust returnest,
Was not spoken of the soul.*

*Not enjoyment, and not sorrow,
Is our destined end or way;
But to act, that each to-morrow
Find us farther than to-day.*

*Art is long, and Time is fleeting,
And our hearts, though stout
and brave,
Still, like muffled drums, are
beating
Funeral marches to the grave.*

*In the world's broad field of
battle,*

*In the bivouac of Life,
Be not like dumb, driven cattle!
Be a hero in the strife!*

*Trust no Future, howe'er
pleasant!
Let the dead Past bury its dead!
Act,— act in the living Present!
Heart within, and God o'erhead!*

*Lives of great men all remind us
We can make our lives sublime,
And, departing, leave behind us
Footprints on the sands of time;*

*Footprints, that perhaps
another,
Sailing o'er life's solemn main,
A forlorn and shipwrecked
brother,
Seeing, shall take heart again.*

*Let us, then, be up and doing,
With a heart for any fate;
Still achieving, still pursuing,
Learn to labor and to wait.*

Henry Wadsworth Longfellow
Deceased 24 March 1882 (aged 75)
Cambridge, United States of America, Earth

FIVE

To laugh often and much; to win
the respect of intelligent people and
the affection of children; to earn the
appreciation of honest critics and
endure the betrayal of false friends;
to appreciate beauty, to find the
best in others; to leave the world
a little better; whether by a healthy
child, a garden patch or a redeemed
social condition; to know even one
life has breathed easier because you
have lived.
This is the meaning of success.

Ralph Waldo Emerson
Deceased 27 April 1882 AD (aged 78)
Concord, United States of America, Earth

Instead of the typical door, today the entrance to Mess Hall 1 was a heavy, velvet-like red curtain partially tied open to reveal a lavish setup inside. The Hall had been impressively rearranged into a fine dining establishment. The bar, kitchen and facilities were clustered right at the entrance. The fancy black-and-white tiled floor was cool to the soles of the feet and pleasing to the eye. The intricate tilework was interspersed with all sorts of colored gems, creating a seamless mosaic, distinct and interesting no matter what particular spot you happened to examine. Many types of exotic flowers were used to decorate the room, grown for months in the gardens just for today. The flowers made the air smell fresh and sweet.

Further in, the space opened into a very large ballroom sealed in on three sides with what appeared to be floor-to-ceiling glass windows. The room seemed to be set atop a cliff whatever side you peered out. The wall to the west depicted the sparkling turquoise coast of Lanikai, Oahu, in Hawaii. There was another smaller island nearby, lazing in the distance. It was a pristine, tranquil beach with no one in sight, just waves upon waves upon waves. If you got close to the wall you could actually hear the gulls' cries in your ears, and feel the cool ocean breeze on your face. The wall to the east looked across the battlements of Castillo San Cristóbal, around the city of Old San Juan, in the

State of Puerto Rico. The bleached, bone-white graves of the cemetery at the base of the high stone walls of the fort glowed brightly in the unrelenting tropical sun. The sanctuary showed the typical Latin reverence for death; the meticulous bastion of bone kept so close to the violent waves of the ocean. If you leaned close enough to the wall you could hear the crash of the surf ricocheting like cannon fire off the heavy stone battlements.

Running about four minutes late and rushing into the room, Lincoln didn't notice these or any of the other multitude of cool effects. The guests were mostly gathered closer to the third glass wall, where tables and seats had been set up and were already collecting plates, cups, and well-dressed people.

About a quarter of the 25-30 guests were standing in rapt attention around Ford, undoubtedly privy to an involved story starring the man himself.

"Lincoln!" his brother shouted loudly from across the room. "You're late!"

The crowd erupted in a spontaneous roar with Ford's exclamation, cheering for their old friend.

The 8 guests of honor were allowed to invite one person each to the luncheon. In addition, Captain Kennedy was there, along with some other more notable retired crew members, some of the remarkable singers and musicians who were going to be performing later, three great poets, two historians, and several other distinguished scientists and varied geniuses. Most of the crowd were dear friends of the Zeta Alpha generation, each guest a very interesting and accomplished person in their own right. It was, inarguably, an older crowd when it came down to it. A team of young faces dressed in matching yellow attire (the twenty year olds, happily volunteering for duty) skirted throughout the crowd, acting as waiters and waitresses, bartenders, and even food staff for the event.

There was a space next to Helen when Lincoln found her, standing with some other dear friends around a round, shiny black table that rose seamlessly from the floor. She looked absolutely radiant. Her gown was diaphanous, glistening like paper-thin liquid gold was cast around her body, caught lightly at the waist by a silver gossamer thread. Her thick black hair was held up high with more of the silver webbing, showing off her regal neck and the sculpted cut of her shoulders and collar bone.

Lincoln drank in all of her majesty as he slowly moved towards her. When their eyes finally met, he looked her up and down once more, his eyes letting her know how good she looked, before slowly moving back up to her coy, waiting smile. Lincoln slowly sauntered towards her and kissed her on the cheek. Then, with a cock of his head, he took her and swept her off her feet, passionately kissing her on the lips just like one of those old movies—much to her pleasant surprise, while the rest of the table hooted and hollered. With a sly smile Lincoln greeted the rest of his friends standing around them. Many in the near vicinity also came to say hello, hugs and kisses all around.

The party quickly slipped into a comfortable reunion of old friends. The Ship assumed the role of head bartender, monitoring the level of each guest's cup and instructing the staff on everyone's particular preferences. The vibrant young waiters and waitresses buzzed around the crowd with platters of different appetizers and personalized drink orders. First among the platters of hors d'oeuvres to appear was a sweet pepper pâte spread on a thin cracker, with spicy roasted seeds on top for crunch. Next were large wedges of peppers of all colors and flavors laden with a salty sauce made of eggplant, olives, and capers. Last but not least were tiny, very peculiar peppers marbled in a rainbow of colors, stuffed with some sort of nutty paste. It was all quite tasty.

"I'm quite sorry, ladies and gentlemen," a man's voice intruded loudly.

Tall Captain Kennedy stood in front of the group, his broad smile showing that he was really not sorry at all. Today his forty fifth birthday, and dapper in his *Captain's Red,* Kennedy certainly looked the part.

"Like you, I would love to continue just enjoying ourselves, but first we have a little bit of business to attend to!"

The crowd booed sarcastically then laughed at themselves. Kennedy smiled then stood seriously before them, playing his role.

"Ladies and gentlemen … after hundreds of years in space and generations of research, we have managed to create some downright wondrous things in our farms. Today, of course, is about the celebration of the Zeta Alpha generation—our dear friends and mentors—but we also have a very special treat for everyone…"

Kennedy smiled widely.

"An *official entry of special merit* into the annals of the Ship! Today, ladies and gentlemen, I am proud to formally introduce to you *Salk's Pepper,* which you have already been enjoying."

With that, two of the biggest twenty-year-olds swept in a long silver tray on which a veritable rainbow of peppers were presented: yellows, oranges, reds, greens, purples, browns, and even black. The edge of the tray was ringed with more of the peculiarly marbled baby peppers. Some of the peppers on the platter were huge, but some were very small. They came in a large range of sizes and shapes, from plump bells to skinny little fingers.

"Ladies and gentlemen…at this moment I am very proud to introduce Salk, Zeta Alpha, who is going to explain to us what's so cool about *Salk's Pepper*."

The crowd burst into raucous applause. Salk, literally one of the shortest people in the room, emerged from the crowd with a sheepish yet entirely content smile. Dressed in a baby-pepper-rainbow shirt, his silver hair trimmed short and neat, he looked like a child next to the tall Captain. The applause swelled as Salk stood there awkwardly, Lincoln leading the charge to a standing ovation.

"Thank you, thank you," said Salk, still smiling, his arms urging them to take their seats. "Please—sit down, people!"

Salk began when they quieted.

"I've spent a good portion of my life fascinated with *Capsicum*, a genus of flowering plant in the nightshade family *Solanaceae*. Peppers similar to these were cultivated natively almost 10,000 years ago in North and South America! We know that the Mayan and Aztec cultures used peppers to flavor cocoa drinks. American Indians used ground chillies as a topical stimulant and analgesic. By more modern times, the pepper had spread virtually everywhere, and was cultivated worldwide…a key element in many types of regional cuisines. Indeed, by the end of the Second Age, capsaicin, the chemical which makes peppers spicy, was even being aerosolized—used by governments for 'nonlethal riot control' and 'non-violent incapacitation.' Those crazy fools…"

Salk walked over to the long tray of peppers. He grabbed two large ones, one mostly yellow and one mostly red, then lobbed them into the crowd with a playful smile. Next, Salk tossed a solid green one over his shoulder, caught by someone in the front row. Grabbing two more, Salk turned to face the crowd. Looking for a fair distribution, he tossed one to the far right of the crowd, which hadn't gotten any love. Smiling wide, Salk threw the last one, shiny purple-black, to Lincoln—a high toss that only his brother could catch.

"Peppers come in all shapes, colors and sizes," Salk continued academically, "yet they all originate from just five species, pretty closely related from a genetic standpoint. In North America they were mild, usually the plump red or green bell peppers we're still accustomed to eating. Yet, these peppers are closely related to all of the piquant varieties: jalapeños and the banana peppers, the green bird's eye, anchos, cayennes… red chillies, habaneros. It's actually pretty confusing, since many of the "types" of chillies are produced by harvesting the peppers of the same plant at different stages. Some peppers are sweet, almost fruity, while others can be bitter. And of course some can be very spicy. Peppers are extremely versatile, too. They can be eaten raw or cooked in many types of ways, as a main dish or a side. You can chop them in a salad or cook them stir-fry, roast them whole or in pieces, chop and incorporate into sauces and salsas, use them in stews. The spice paprika is made from peppers. Peppers have been preserved in jams, dried, and pickled. Extracts can be made into hot sauces. And—most critically now—peppers are just plain great for the human body. Among the nutrients they provide are Vitamins C, A, K, E, B6, Potassium, Manganese, Thiamin, Niacin, Folate, Magnesium and Copper, not to mention six carotenoids! Peppers can also be a rich source of sulfur-containing compounds, protecting against cancer. I mean, wow…right? The pepper is one amazing vegetable. Give it up for the pepper, people!"

The crowd laughed and then cheered sarcastically, which only made them laugh again.

"The Spanish conquistadores were the ones to first introduce peppers to Spain and thus Europe, then into the Philippines, where they spread into the rest of Asia, including the real culinary heavyweights, China and India. Hot peppers were particularly appreciated not only for their ability to enliven monotonous diets, but also for some of the digestive effects of capsicum—they make you sweat, helping to cool you off in the heat. *All of the cuisines of Latin America re-*

volved around peppers. Spanish cuisine pairs the chili with garlic and olive oil, plus chorizo—spicy sausages made with picante peppers. Peppers are essential ingredients in the cuisines of India, Ethiopia, Southern China, and Thailand, among others. The pepper really is one versatile vegetable!"

"All of this got me thinking … Peppers were so prolific, nutritious AND highly versatile, yet all of these benefits comes from just five highly related species. So—and this is over fifty years ago, mind you—I decided that there was a way to combine and catalogue the totality of *Capsicum* genomes in a sort of genetic hierarchy of outcomes. One of the great things about peppers—and most fruits and vegetables, really—is their ability to communicate through color. You see, the colors of vegetables communicate the concentrations of nutrients and certain other compounds. The skin of the mature red bell pepper, for example, has three times the level of beta carotene than a green, immature, one—it's the same thing that also makes carrots and pumpkins orange—and significantly higher levels of vitamins A and C, also helping the deep red color. All of this inspired me to build a genetic compendium of pepper genes, organized by nutrition then quickly branching into categories of heat, taste, function, then several other variables pertinent to the farms like size, growing time and yield."

Salk shrugged.

"Basically, I combined and then organized the gene sequences of *Capsicum annums, Capsicum baccatums, Capsicum chinense* and *Capsicum pubescens*, and a few others, all in one master plant. About thirty years ago I started seeing some really promising results. Once I figured out which genes were tied to color and taste and heat, I began to play around. And once I began to show actionable results, I was given a whole quarter-acre of the farms for my experiments!"

Salk walked back over to the tray and gathered many of the small, rainbow-marbled peppers. He began handing them out to the people closest to him.

"Here's the real secret. We've engineered these peppers to be extremely malleable during a certain developmental period in their life cycle. Then we developed several ways to trigger the various phenotypic changes. So, for example, if you grow this pepper in low water conditions, you eventually get a small, potent, nutrient-rich, red pepper. In high sun they get much bigger, with a much larger range of possible outcomes. Soil content can affect the peppers too, as can other external stimuli. I've noticed a difference in taste and texture of identical plants fertilized by bees only one day apart! Therefore—theoretically—a farmer slash chef can adjust the taste of his or her peppers to very exacting specifications: mild to instant heat;

sour to fruity in taste; dull or bright; different levels of smokiness; even skin texture. Even further, the Ship could proscribe a certain pepper as part of a balanced diet. But most importantly, a pepper that contains this genetic heritage is perfect for a new planet! It can quickly evolve to suit many types of climates and environments, in many beneficial ways for colonists."

Salk smiled proudly.

"The peppers we've developed could be very useful to many people one day. My greatest hope is that current and future generations of scientists continue this research. We are all standing on the shoulders of many countless others. This is nothing but a hi-tech version of what Gregor Mendel was doing with his pea plants on Earth in the 1850s, almost a thousand years ago. The process applied here is equally applicable to the entire family *Solanoideae,* a subfamily of the flowering plant family Solanaceae—the nightshades that share the same great diversity of habitat, morphology and ecology as *Capsicum.* So, tomatoes, potatoes, eggplants, tomatillos, the gooseberries, *Physalis peruviana,* Chinese lanterns—there are 98 genera and thousands of species which can be combined and optimized in the same way. You could probably even do this with other flowering plant families. There could be great potential there since these plants naturally produce many types of alkaloids, a secondary metabolite with pharmaceutical benefits."

Salk sighed for a second, then smiled widely, animated.

"It's more than ripe! Someone please do this work!"

The crowd broke into applause once more.

"That's enough from me, everybody. Thank you once again. I couldn't have done this without the support of all of you and many others … some still alive but most no longer with us. I would especially like to thank my sisters and brothers and this great Ship of ours."

Salk paused, still smiling, as he took on a more formal air.

"Everyone please rise for a moment so that the dining tables can be set up. As our main lunch course please enjoy roasted *Salk Peppers* stuffed with a variety of different fillings. Each one should taste differently, and hopefully delicious. Special thanks to Master Chef Hazen and the kitchen crew for all the help. They do the real magic. You're going to have to ask the servers to help you with the particulars—the peppers have been stuffed with all sorts of grains, figs, nuts, and so forth."

At this point everyone had risen. All of the tables had been cleared and they, along with the chairs people had been just sitting on, began to melt back into the floor. Shiny black octagonal tables rose regularly along the north wall, with seats rising around them.

The lights dimmed gradually, but spotlights now shone onto the tables, lending an even more sophisticated vibe.

Lincoln and Helen grabbed a table. With them were Dorothy and Oz (his sister and brother), in matching formal suits of bright blue, Amelia (his sister), in a beautiful purple gown and her 40-something date, Melville, surprisingly also in purple. The final two seats were taken by Avi and Mega, dear old friends.

"I always knew that our Salkie would turn out pretty good," Lincoln said with a broad smile, breaking the ice.

Everyone laughed.

"Yes—*we all* turned out good," Dorothy stressed, "Salkie is a great one though," she added happily.

Dorothy and Oz had been an inseparable pair their entire lives. It's not like anyone really inquired about the pair's sexual proclivities in the first place—in space pretty much anything goes, after all. No one was genetically related (so the inhabitants of the Ship were significantly past that particular taboo), and everyone was sterile anyway, no longer capable of creating by sexual reproduction. Officially married, a rarity these days, Dorothy and Oz were also *that* couple. It was the type of connection where the loving pair-bond was evident just by the way their bodies were always positioned; a casually laid hand here, a private, hilarious secret whispered in the ear there.

The food came out just then, a plate set down in front of each of them. Every golden plate had a large, elegantly presented stuffed pepper which was actually re-constructed from two different halves. One half of Lincoln's was a deep, glistening, multi-faceted red, the other half bright yellow like a lemon with orange polka dots. He split his portion with Helen, gaining a taste of her dish: speckled green-on-green, with an orange partner with purple-black tiger stripes. As advertised, the food was delicious. There were many wonderful color combinations of peppers, all with different fillings. Everyone shared theirs with the others around them.

Captain Kennedy's amplified voice again cut through the din.

"Ladies and gentlemen … It is my pleasure to introduce to you the wonderful woman who is going to sing for us now. Please welcome, Lata!"

A middle aged woman began to perform without further ado, two other musicians accompanying her on obsidian keyboards that had risen up smoothly from the floor in front of them. It was exceptional R & B; soft, moody music which was extremely lush at the same time.

Looking up from his plate—a much needed break from the second onslaught of peppers to come out of the kitchen—Lincoln stared at the busy scene on the wall closest to them. A flash of data in his eyes told him that it had been taken from New York City, in the sunset of the Second Age. From their high vantage point they looked to be at the top of a tall building, amid a block of still-sparkling eco-towers in the Heights of Brooklyn, looking towards the old city. Unlike the still-sparkling buildings on this side, a haphazard mix of dilapidated towers stood in a messy skeleton across the dark, swollen river. Some to the north still glittered, but the further south you looked the buildings became more and more rusty and broken. The two worn humps of concrete sticking out of the murky water were once the "Brooklyn Bridge," a prompt in his eyes told him. They'd only lasted in that spot because the concrete was entirely worthless. The other tall bridges that used to lie further north had been scavenged away long ago, metal always valuable.

At that moment, leaving from the top of the tall building next to them was a shiny green tram, suspended below a cable extending from a tall spire at the top of the building. Gaining speed quickly, the green box, emblazoned with a large 5, quickly slid down, soon far from them. Following the cable with his eyes, Lincoln saw that there was a sort of central landing place far cross the wide river. Several other brightly colored trams descended down from there, down to the top of the high walls that defended the old city from the murky water. Boats of all sizes also busily crossed the river. Looking even further south, that's when Lincoln saw her—Lady Liberty! The great statue was still holding on, mostly keeping up appearances. The problem was that the old green lady was waist deep in murky sludge.

A squeeze of his thigh then quick advance towards his crotch immediately pulled Lincoln out of it. Turning, he found Helen smiling at him while she shook her head. Everyone else had left the table.

"There ya go again," she said

"Where'd everyone else go?" asked Lincoln, confused.

Helen raised one of her eyebrows before answering. "Seriously? Well, I'm pretty sure that Dorothy and Oz just went to find a room somewhere … those two are absolutely amazing. Amelia and her man Melville—who'd have thunk?—are on the dance floor, and the Betas saw an opening with Salk."

Lincoln shook his head, sighing deeply.

"I wish I could stop time right here. It's a pretty perfect moment, don't you think? It's so happy here, with all our friends around us. And you're still so beautiful…"

Lincoln looked down at his unfinished plate, an uncomfortable expression working across his face.

It was a while until he spoke again.

"Oz and Dorothy have it so easy, you know."

Helen looked at him intently, desperately wanting Lincoln to look at her, to add the power of his eyes to what he was expressing. Yet stubbornly, Lincoln continued to stare down at his plate.

"Being able to go out together, like that … I envy that very much. It would be so much easier. Helen … I love you so much."

His words were very soft when he finished, but their effect on her was immediate. Helen quickly got up from her chair then sat right back down in Lincoln's lap, an embrace he couldn't deny.

"I love you too Lincoln."

He looked at her finally, smiling but still very sad.

"Envy?" said Helen with a fake-astonished smile. "In the great Captain Lincoln!?! You better not let the kids find out. It would totally ruin your rep!"

Lincoln sat stone-faced. It was another few moments before he broke the silence.

"Do you ever wish we got married?"

"Huh?" Helen was the confused one this time. "That's a pretty massive jump in conversation, Link."

Yet he said it again, in the same serious voice.

"Do you ever wish we got married?" After another tense moment he continued, "We never really talked about it. But you are the love of my life. I've known that for such a long time. And some people really like it…marriage."

Helen smiled radiantly before kissing him deeply on the lips.

"Lincoln, you know I don't care about that crap! I studied it for years! Marriage is an entirely *man-made* institution—not *woman-made*. It's nothing more than a development which typically occurs in societies under certain conditions, with both negative and positive outcomes. I always just loved you, Link. Who cares about anything else but that?"

Lincoln sighed deeply, physically relaxing into Helen with her words. He loved her presence weighing on him heavily. She loved being in his arms, especially in such a vulnerable, intimate moment. They fell into a contented, happy silence, living a private moment together surrounded by their best friends in the world.

Helen's head resting on his shoulder, Lincoln looked out into the now mostly standing crowd. He found Ford quickly through his loud, easy laugh. His brother was always surrounded by people, always telling a story. Lincoln admired Ford's face as he talked; all of the little smiles and grimaces that he fit with his words just the right way, plus the way he controlled his hands, his whole body really, to help him communicate his ideas to others. Lincoln found Amelia in the crowd next, his

tall sister, always his equal in both competitiveness and seriousness, and still as unflappable as ever. Yet Lincoln could tell by her smirk that his sister was really enjoying herself—dancing circles around poor young Mel. Dorothy and Oz were dancing too now, in their own little world. The man of the hour Salk was still standing by the tables receiving congratulations, but at this point he was listening far more than he was speaking. His brother still had the hawkish, questioning look that Lincoln so admired. Emma, Lincoln's small sister, was tough to spot, but her loud voice soon gave away her location too. She was small, yet fierce. Similar to Salk, Emma carried that inquisitive squint in her eyes too, but hers was more confrontational, more in-your-face. She showed it off even now, loudly arguing with the person next to her, pretending to be angry but clearly (mostly) playing around.

Looking around the room once, and then twice, Lincoln suddenly realized it: one of his favorite people in the whole world was a no-show! *Where the heck was his other sister?*

"Hey Helen—have you seen Sojie around at all today?"

Helen shook her head.

"Hmm."

Using his eyes, Lincoln opened up a channel with his sister.

Lincoln: *Hey, sis. What's up with you? Not seeing you at OUR party.*

She responded close to instantly.

Sojourner: *Sorry, love. I've been here in Medical since early this morning. I never intended to go to the luncheon. That's why I messaged you this morning about later.*

Sojourner: *We have a few first timers, and, well, I can't miss a second of any of it! We still have three more babies to go.*

Lincoln: *Fine. I'm coming to you!*

Lincoln squeezed Helen tight.

"I'm gonna stop by and see Sojie in the Medical Ward. It's on the way to the Classrooms anyway. Do you want to come with me?"

Helen thought about it for a moment before she shook her head.

"No, my love. You go. Take your time. Maybe go to the gardens, smell the new roses that just came in. Do whatever it is you that you need to do. I have to help get ready for later."

They kissed passionately once more before Helen hopped off of Lincoln. He stood, then adjusted his shirt.

"Okay . . . So, I'm going to be with the young ones for about an hour, then we have a little block scheduled for just the 8 of us, right before the party. I'll see you at 6 PM, on the dot?"

The way he said it made it seem like a very serious question. Lincoln patiently waited for an answer, staring at her with his big, brown, puppy-dog eyes. For a moment it felt like they were young lovers again.

Helen answered him breathlessly, like a school girl asked out on a date for the very first time: "I wouldn't miss it for anything, Captain Lincoln."

Lincoln smiled at her gratefully before turning and sauntering away, the party now in full swing. Indeed, from the look of some of the others it seemed like the party was just getting started.

The Song of the Wandering Aengus
(Last verse)

Though I am old with wandering
Through hollow lands and hilly lands,
I will find out where she has gone,
And kiss her lips and take her hands;
And walk among long dappled grass,
And pluck till time and times are done,
The silver apples of the moon,
The golden apples of the sun.

William Butler Yeats
Deceased 28 January 1939 AD (aged 73)
Dublin, Ireland, Earth

SIX

They give birth astride of a grave,
the light gleams an instant, then it's
night once more.

Samuel Beckett
Deceased 22 December 1989 AD (aged 83)
Paris, France, Earth

He was still far down the hallway from his destination, but Lincoln could hear a woman screaming in anguish. It shot chills straight down his spine.

"Now that's some real pain," he whispered to himself.

Working his way through the wide, permanent tunnels that stretched around the farms, for a moment Lincoln thought of escaping for a quick respite to a favorite, quiet spot in the gardens. Time pushed back though, as did the thought of seeing his sister.

With a resolute clench of his jaw and the shake of the head, Lincoln kept going.

Quickly enough he was there. Bypassing the first closed door marked *MEDICAL*, Lincoln walked through the second, open door which led into the large room. Today, however, the space was configured as a small observation deck, cut off from the main delivery room by a clear, glass-like partition. A large group of people stood in front of it in the otherwise simple, white-walled room, staring through the glass into the busy delivery room beyond. Audio from the birthing area was piped in, creating the sense that the wall wasn't even there.

Lincoln moved to the only open space in front of the clear wall. The man and woman directly to his left nodded politely and smiled, which Lincoln acknowledged with a quick nod and smile of his own. To the right of him, Lincoln was happy to find that the extremely short, more salt-than-pepper-haired woman staring utterly transfixed at the developing scene was his sister. He gave her a gentle poke with his elbow.

"Link!" Sojourner exclaimed far too loudly, causing the other people in the room to turn and stare. She apologized with a sheepish shrug and her wide smile.

Sojie and Lincoln hugged for a good while before topping it off with kisses on both cheeks, which Lincoln had to bend down very low to accomplish. They clung to each other, one of her arms slung around his waist and the other on his stomach, his right arm comfortably resting across her shoulders.

Not wanting to disturb the rest of the room, they switched back to the private channel:

Lincoln: *Hey, kiddo. I've missed you.*

Sojourner: *Ditto. Looking sharp too, love.*

Lincoln: *Thanks. You look tired. How are you holding up?*

Sojourner: *Holding up the best I can, I guess. Trying to stay busy. I've been with the mothers since very early this morning—answering questions, making sure they were comfortable, doing whatever was needed for the most part … that is, until they kicked me out right before the first birth. How rude!*

Soujourner: *I'm tired though—you've got that right. I haven't been sleeping well, for a variety of reasons.*

Still holding each other, they watched as four attendants covered head-to-toe in white prepped equipment and ran diagnostics, buzzing around but not disturbing the young woman lying on the table in the center of the room. The walls of the bay were ablaze with all sorts of medically related images. The woman was resting quietly with her eyes closed, which relieved Lincoln mightily.

Lincoln: *Ditto for me with the sleep. I haven't had*

a good night's sleep in months! I'm getting pretty tired of being tired all the time…Anyway, I have to go meet the young ones next, and for the first time ever I'm not looking forward to it. It's supposed to be one of their first conversations about life and death. Honestly, I'm not even sure where to start…

Sojourner gave him a squeeze and they made eye contact again, smiling at each other for a moment before looking back into the delivery room.

Sojourner: *Yeesh. Five-year-olds aren't meant to think about death, let alone have any sort of conversation about it. What do you think…should protocol be changed?*

Lincoln: *I leave that for people smarter than me to decide. But, on the other hand, I am a fan of full disclosure in just about every instance I can think of.*

Lincoln: *You can't protect kids from life, and dying is a fact of life. It's better for the kids to know these facts, and experience them, than not, regardless of whether they can fully appreciate or comprehend what's being said to them. We came out pretty darn good, didn't we?*

Sojourner: *Yes, we did.*

Suddenly the woman let out a full-throated scream, writhing in agony on the bed.

Lincoln: *Damn! They need to give that girl some drugs.*

Sojourner: *No! You'd really like this girl, Link. She's a real trooper, just like you and maybe even more stubborn! She decided quite some time ago that she was going to take NOTHING. No drugs, not even a low-dose anesthetic. She wants to "really feel what it feels like!"*

Sojourner: *Let me tell you this, Lincoln … I was a surrogate mother four times myself. The thought of not taking any drugs never once crossed my mind! It's a bit insane, really. Right now that young woman is feeling more pain than you or I can even imagine! But life comes in all sorts, bless her heart. We've learned that first hand. Some types of people need a little pain in their lives, for whatever darn reason. It helps them feel.*

The girl screamed again, a primal, blood-curdling sound.

Lincoln: *Well she's certainly feeling something now.*

Sojourner: *It's getting close. You can tell by the scan, there.*

She pointed towards one of the largest screens on the wall of the other room. Indeed, in that very moment the room seemed to explode in activity, the four attendants rushing to surround the woman. She was on her back, her feet planted on the table with her knees up. Her stomach was swollen and she was sweating profusely, the moisture causing a graduated purple-to-red color change in the blanket that was draped over her. The blanket itself was the same design that everyone owned. Your blanket was your only real possession aboard the Ship, in a tangible sense at least. Everyone's light blanket was the same: the inner core a weave of several hi-tech materials with a disposable (and hence cleanable) outer cover made of extremely warm, stretchy microfibers. The rudimentary neural net of a blanket was like that of a square starfish. Lincoln's and Helen's large blanket, having been fused together from two smaller ones long ago, would stay afloat in the air when one of them got out of bed, slowly flapping around in the air, hovering for an instant before reluctantly pulling itself back in towards the warmth of the remaining partner. The still-screaming woman's blanket looked very different now, however. It was tethered securely to the long edges of the table and stretched taut, holding tight around the peak of her swollen belly. Her arms were held tight against her body underneath the blanket; pinned, useless and helpless.

She took a giant gulp of air and then wailed again; long, in complete anguish. It looked like her belly was undulating, though it was hard to tell since she was breathing so heavily. Three of the attendants crowded below her legs while a fourth woman stayed above, giving instruction and encouragement. Amidst the prolonged, painful screams, only the clinical, most zoomed-in screen of the action showed the real change. Something began to emerge from the woman, round and red. It seemed to be stuck there for too long—more than a minute, the woman still screaming her fucking head off—until most of the head was out. Then, with what was more like a long angry grunt from the young woman, the baby seemed to just fall right out, expertly caught in the arms of an attendant, bloody and red and, in a few seconds, screaming *its* fucking head off.

Silent the whole time, the crowd audibly exhaled before breaking into applause.

The umbilical cord was cut and the attendant quickly cleaned the squirming little thing. She brought it to the woman first: baby's first kiss, a blessing from Mama, letting the exhausted woman hold it for a spell. After some time the attendant brought the child close to the wall, giving the small crowd a view of the tiny, speckled-red baby which had just emerged—the newest living person on the U.S.N.A.S. *Hope Eternal.*

"Baby number six, female," the attendant spoke happily, "Zeta Rho generation." She turned and left with the newborn, disappearing into another room across the far side of the Medical Ward. "Baby number six" (or maybe simply just *Six*) would be her name

for some time to come. According to Ship protocol, babies were not named at birth; the underlying idea echoing many cultures from Earth but mostly basic pragmatism. Names were given later, when the child first began to show a personality, and by the nursery crew, the people who knew them the best. Often the Ship would generate a list of names from Earth history or fiction that the child would hopefully grow to appreciate based on a combination of current societal factors, the child's genetic profile and developing personality—even the child's likely future proclivities and fields of interest. Usually one of the nursery crew would pick something they liked from the list, though not always.

A name was important, at least to some. Sometimes people—young people in particular—needed something to fixate on. Being genetically designed and implanted in a surrogate mother, parents and background were eliminated from the picture. Yet some people still needed something to attach their identities to. For Lincoln, his name had been a steady beacon of light, a steadying force that was always there in the background. Abraham Lincoln—he had found out at age seven—had been a very great man: a true leader, compassionate and smart when his people needed him the most, but also a great thinker whose views evolved over time then hardened with wisdom, a man finally murdered by people who disagreed with his ideas. Captain Lincoln had found solace in his name and the person he shared it with, and hoped that baby Six would eventually have a name that she'd grow to love too.

"I need to get going," Lincoln whispered to his sister, the rest of the crowd already having broken into light chatter. "It's almost time for me to meet with the kids over in Classroom 1. Do you want come along? Some moral support wouldn't hurt…and they all sure love you. I have a feeling that this is going to be rough."

"No, Link," Sojie apologized, the empathy plainly written all across her expressive face. "Sorry, but I really can't. It's not just that I made promises to all of these women…I need to watch them all, to see all the new ones just once. It's just something that I need to do, for myself."

She smiled up at him.

"I'll see you in a little while though, big brother? Just the 8 of us again—like old times?"

"Wouldn't miss it for the world," Lincoln promised with a wide smile.

They hugged, another long embrace, and kissed again. Then Lincoln turned and left, leaving his sister once again standing nervously in the observation deck peering anxiously into the delivery room.

SEVEN

Our death is not an end if we can
live on in our children
and the younger generation.
For they are us, our bodies are only
wilted leaves on the tree of life.

Albert Einstein
Deceased 18 April 1955 AD (aged 76)
Princeton, United States of America, Earth

The thing that immediately struck Lincoln was how empty the familiar room felt. Classroom 1 was the mirror image of Classroom 2, yet the smaller desks and miniature people sitting silently made it feel much larger than the older kids' otherwise identical area. The room was dark aside from the flashing deskscreens, but also devoid of any other adults besides the two teachers at the front. The little ones were fully immersed in whatever they were watching, thoroughly enjoying the sounds now ringing in their ears. Their laughter rang out on occasion, choruses of joy that punctuated the eerie quiet. Unlike the other Classroom, there was no Teacher's console here either, though they could have one in no time if they wanted it. Diana, Helen's sister and Lincoln's longtime friend, sat on a low, comfortable bench, eye to eye with the children. A younger teacher named Ashira sat next to Diana in the lotus position, her eyes closed, monitoring the children's progress.

At the age of five, education mainly consisted of interaction with other people: play and structured class time as a group, many visits from adults, time spent with the older children, and then exposure to various realities of Ship life, in that order. On most days the classroom was a whirling dervish of activity. On some days, the walls were completely covered in a crazy hodgepodge of art made by all of them, the session usually led by two or three contemporary artists visiting for the afternoon; the sum always greater than the parts. On other days, the room was an explosion of shrieks and laughter as the children were regaled by a favorite person's stories, or a science demonstration, or many types of performances of the body, voice, or mind. They had also just begun making music together, cacophonous days led by various musical geniuses as special guests; so far demonstrating some decent parts but still a disaster of a sum. All days were about being curious. All days started with questions and ended with more. All days brought new wonders, not only for the children but for everyone else who was there to see it happen.

It's just so quiet, with the kids plugged-in, thought Lincoln. *They're oblivious to the outside world right now, totally distracted from reality. And I'm supposed to talk to them about life and death?*

Diana pinged Lincoln, who was still standing silently in the dark by the doorway.

Diana: *Captain Lincoln, my dear friend, as usual right on time! As you can see, we, as usual, are not. I know you must be extremely busy today. This is just a demo program, so I am going to cut it right now. We can just start it back up later—the kids won't care.*

All of the screens in the room suddenly went black. The lights quickly adjusted to a brighter setting.

The children looked up in confusion.

"Captain Lincoln!" the little girl nearest to him called out after a few moments. Lincoln was leaning with his back against the door frame, subconsciously trying to channel James Dean.

"Oh Captain!" another cried out.

"Captain Lincoln! Captain Lincoln!"

The children bounced in their seats, overjoyed

to have found their old friend. As they called out his name it created a high pitched babble which echoed throughout the room.

"Good afternooooon, Captain Linc-ennn," asserted Diana. She used the slow, cutting, super-enunciated (and universal) voice used by all teachers to shepherd young ones.

The children immediately sat straight at their desks, trained well, totally on cue. "Good afternooooon, Captain Linc-ennn," they enthusiastically spoke as a group, with Teacher's exact enunciation.

"Good afternoon, children." Lincoln smiled, at least sounding confident as he slowly moved to the front of the room, 8 sets of adorable eyes following his every move. His stomach felt queasy again. The gurgling, empty stabs of pain in his stomach had become a gassy, bloated concrete mixer after eating too much, too fast. And peppers too! Gritting his teeth, Lincoln tried his best to ignore it.

"Happy birthday!" he exclaimed when he stood at the front of the class, his hands clasped together.

"Happy birthday to YOU!" the girl closest to him said as she pointed at him.

The children all laughed, delighted.

Lincoln spoke deliberately. "I know you all know what a special day today is. I saw you watching that program! You are now listening like we listen. You are old enough to start really using your eyes now, too. You are going to learn many great new things."

Lincoln knew to stop right there. Some of those adorable eyes were already starting to glaze over. Anything else pertaining to access and implants and he would lose them to excited daydreams, and lose them fast. Right now Lincoln needed to stay focused like a laser, not an easy task when speaking with a group of young children. *But how do you possibly explain life and death to a five-year-old?*

Lincoln started slowly. "Today is the one day when the life cycle of our Ship is the most clear," he said with a sage nod. "All of the action, so they would say, happens today. You had your surgeries this morning, I see. And by the look of it, all very successful!"

The point earned Lincoln 8 wide smiles, not one with a full contingent of teeth.

"Little ones are being born this very moment which means YOU, my young friends, are no longer the babies of this Ship."

This drove the kids into a frenzy, clapping hands and jumping out of their seats before being shushed by their Teachers.

"The ten-year-olds will start working in the farms today ... They'll be able to walk the gardens and pick food with their own hands. That is a big responsibility. You should ask them about it when you see them!"

Lincoln was on a roll and he knew it.

"The older children? Wait . . . what am I saying? They're not even children anymore! They're adults."

This idea delighted the youngsters.

"They have even greater responsibilities beyond the farms. They get to work in other places, like in the Medical Ward, or in Engineering, or in the Labs, doing research . . . or maybe even the Kitchen, or as a full-time artist or dancer. All sorts of interesting places all over the Ship, working on jobs with other adults."

This was a very general summary. Today the newly minted adults would be placed into various programs and courses of study, some having to do with various Ship systems, but some not. None of the jobs were critical in any real sense—but then again, no jobs were. Their course had been set for hundreds of years, and everything was basically taken care of by the Ship: energy generation, propulsion, shielding, recycling, gravity, and all of the other systems. Food production from farm to table, research, sometimes moving materials in and out of reclamation, and some slight engineering/maintenance were the only jobs that needed actual human hands.

"But I haven't told you anything that you didn't already know, have I?"

"Noooo, Captain Lincoln," they answered, mostly on cue.

"Does anyone know what else happens today?" Lincoln asked.

The question elicited a quick hand. Lincoln pointed to the child closest to him, the precocious little girl who had spoken out earlier.

"There's a big party tonight. HUGE, really. We don't get to stay up ALL night…but we'll be at dinner with everyone, and there's music, and there's dancing, and very exciting things happening." She took her answer very seriously, sounding at least two and a half times her age.

"Yes!" Lincoln said happily. *He could work with that.*

"There IS a big party. Does anybody know why?"

He shook off the first girl, who lowered her hand with a crinkle of her nose, and looked around the room for another volunteer. Another girl raised her hand.

"It's everybody's birthday today," she said, matter-of-factly.

"Exactly," said Lincoln with a wide smile. "There's a huge party tonight because today is everybody's birthday! Your birthday…my birthday…TEACHER's birthdays."

He paused for dramatic effect.

"On this Ship 8 brothers and sisters are born every five years, just like you and your brothers and sisters,

So we have a party! Everyone comes together, and we have fun and celebrate!"

Lincoln could see the point hit home, with satisfaction. These were very smart kids, and the idea of generations was a basic fact of life to them.

"There's something else, too."

Lincoln paused for a second, reflective. His throat was suddenly bone dry. *How do you put this to a five-year-old?*

He spoke gently after a few moments. "Tonight … later tonight, after the party. After you all go to sleep…"

He paused.

"Tonight my brothers and sisters and I are going to die."

Lincoln had been looking directly at a young boy when he said it. The boy's face went from serenely happy to visibly disturbed; his eyes immediately darker, his mouth stuck open dumbly. The excitement that had filled the room only moments ago instantly evaporated, like it had never been there in the first place. The singular remaining feeling was a deep, palpable sadness.

The silence lingered like a tumor. Eventually a slow hand came from a little boy.

"Why die, Captain Lincoln?" he asked timidly. "Why will you die?"

Lincoln searched for exactly the right words.

"Every living thing dies, my son. Everything in nature has its time to live, and then it dies. It's your turn to live. It's my turn to die."

The child persisted. "But why do you have to die *tonight*?"

Still standing in front of the children, Lincoln felt ill. His palms were sweaty yet felt strangely cold at the same time. He quickly wiped them on the back of his pants as he shifted his weight.

"I will die tonight because I choose to."

The child was still visibly confused, so he continued.

"Tonight, I will go to sleep and never wake up. The man, the Captain Lincoln that you love, will be gone."

"But, WHY?" demanded the very first girl.

Lincoln sighed, suddenly tired of reciting the same rationale over and over again. Still, he smiled gently as he spoke it.

"I am an old man and our Ship is very small. We only have food and water and air for a limited number of people, and we need room for the new babies and for everyone else. There just isn't ... enough. So, in a piece of wisdom passed down from the very first people to set foot on our Ship, we, the very oldest, will die tonight—the night of our eightieth birthday. We know that you are our future, so we give it to you freely."

The mood of the room seemed to improve ever so slightly.

"Captain Lincoln," another little boy asked next, "how will you die?" Normally he was a confident, outgoing boy, but the question came out meekly, mostly fear in the words.

"I will go to sleep and I won't wake up," said Lincoln. When he saw that it wasn't enough he continued, "I will go to sleep. My heart will stop beating and my brain and my body will be dead. YOU will be alive, and Teachers Ashira and Diana will be alive … but I won't be here anymore. Life will go on—for you and for everyone else."

The fear was dissipating now. The children didn't seem as scared. Curiosity gently lifted their angelic faces.

Another girl raised her hand next. "What will happen to your body?"

"We are star-stuff harvesting starlight,[6]" Lincoln answered with a smile. "Believe it or not, we are made from the stars, my child! Every bit of your being is made up of dust that was flung out of the death of some star very far away, very long ago. The atoms that make us, that stardust, have taken shape into more forms than you can ever even begin to imagine. Just like you, I am made of that dust. When I die it no longer belongs to me, right? What was me, my body, will go to reclamation, and this material will go back to the Ship."

Lincoln smiled gently.

"A poet I really love from Earth wrote: *I believe a leaf of grass is no less than the journeywork of the stars.*[7] Well he was right—and far before his time! *I bequeath myself to the dirt to grow from the grass I love. If you want me again look for me under your boot-soles.*"

The thought actually made Lincoln feel better himself. The mood of the room lifted even more.

Totally shattering it, the silent alarm went off again, rattling Lincoln's ears, his eyes overtaken by large blinking text:

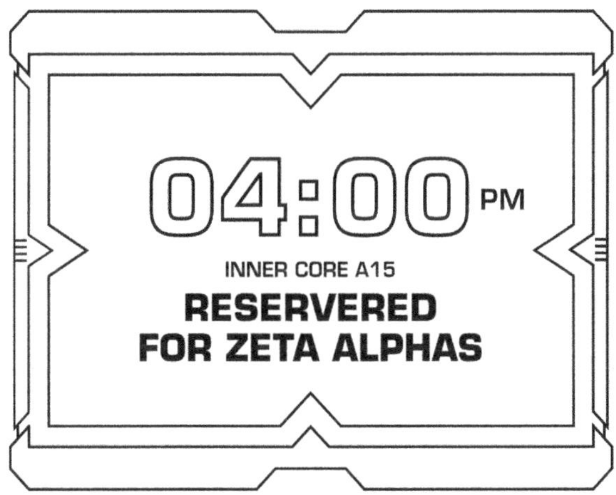

"Shhhhhii... " Lincoln saved himself, the T tucked safely behind his lips.

THIS FUCKING ALARM, he thought, gritting his teeth angrily. *Time is one terrible enemy. It's simple— you just can't win.*

Frowning, Lincoln nodded.

"I need to go now, kiddos," he said softly. "I am very sad to say that, but I have to go meet my sisters and brothers in a few minutes."

Lincoln moved reluctantly from the front of the room, taking slow steps towards the exit. "It's just the 8 of us hanging out for a while before dinner, all of us together one last time, but I don't want to be late…not today."

Lincoln stopped, looking around at the tiny, beautiful people all peering up at him.

"It was my pleasure to speak with all of you. I love each and every one of you very much," he said.

The girl closest to him grabbed his hand.

"I love you Captain Lincoln," she said quietly, in a tooth-missing lisp.

Suddenly the kids were on their feet and swarming all around him, none much higher than a knee.

"We love you Captain Lincoln!" they said. "We love you Captain Lincoln!"

Another child grabbed Lincoln's other hand and the weight of the two small ones soon had him pulled down to one knee, onto their level. Then one of the boys slung an arm around Lincoln's neck, just like they were brothers. Very soon it was a group hug. Lincoln closed his eyes, taking deep breaths. He could feel a warmth envelop him, not just body heat but something else entirely. It was a cleansing feeling; relaxing, almost replenishing. When he was ready, after a long while, Lincoln tried to stand up. The children reacted instantly, *all hands on deck*, pushing and guiding him up with their hands, soon helping Lincoln back to his full, considerably imposing height.

"Thank you," Lincoln said with a laugh. "I really love you guys! I will see you for a little while later tonight, I promise. Enjoy our birthday!"

Lincoln turned and smiled at the two teachers with a deferential nod. Then he exited Classroom 1 for the very last time in his life.

EIGHT

Life is pleasant.
Death is peaceful.
It's the transition that's troublesome.

Isaac Asimov
Deceased 6 April 1992 AD (aged 72)
Brooklyn, United States of America, Earth

When Lincoln left the Classroom his head was spinning. As quickly as the group hug had seemed to fill his emotional tank, the tranquility drained out like there was a gaping hole in the bottom. It was like he'd overloaded his system, too much emotion at once. His physical symptoms had also come back full-force, no longer ignorable. His stomach heaved like an angry ocean, his mouth suddenly filled with far too much saliva. Luckily the hallway was empty—a rare thing this close to the farms. Lincoln stopped walking altogether, leaning a hand on the black wall. His other hand gripped his forehead like a vise, trying to fight pressure with pressure.

Shit, he thought. *Hold it together, man! Just hold it together.*

Lincoln had worked his entire conscious life to be a steady, stoic and unaffected man, but this finely honed edifice began to crumble like an elaborate castle carved out of sand. The rises and falls of the conversation, the pure radiance and love of the group hug—all of it had touched the core of his being. This great emotion had flooded his system with a blissful high, but the rebound was almost as great.

Suddenly the normally dominant, rational part of Lincoln's brain was completely and totally locked out of his body. He no longer had any control. He felt sick, old, and so very tired. Weak in the knees, he was doing all that he could just to stand. The support of the smooth black wall was the only thing that kept him on his feet.

He didn't know how long he stayed there, holding on just steps outside the door of the Classroom. Yet after a while the sound of footsteps hastened, coming towards him from around the bend of the hallway.

Lincoln closed his eyes as he clenched his jaw tight, at war with his emotions. *Composure*, he thought. *Come on … Hold it together, man!*

At this point it was inevitable. The footsteps, now accompanied with loud, excited voices, were approaching quickly. They were probably right around the bend—and all Lincoln wanted to do was curl into a ball.

Slowly, Lincoln straightened to his full height before he turned towards the people. He didn't want to. He didn't want anyone to see him like this, just on the cusp of a breakdown. But he couldn't just ignore them—that would be far worse. His pride—plus a lifetime's reputation—was at stake.

But Lincoln just couldn't face them. He was broken.

Shaking his head, literally his whole body quaking, Captain Lincoln asked the Ship for a mighty big favor and it was granted. Digging his fingernails like claws high into the black skin of the wall closest to him, he slowly ripped down on it. Like a huge sheet of metal paper, the material separated itself from the wall. Spinning once carefully, Lincoln wrapped himself in it, then secured it back to the wall, trapping himself in it like a bubble in the wallpaper. The outside hallway thickened itself out after a few seconds, straight and smooth like nothing had happened.

From the inside of his impromptu cocoon it was at first dark and very warm. In a moment the walls grew lighter, glowing all around him in a soft, comforting blue light. The space was small but bigger than

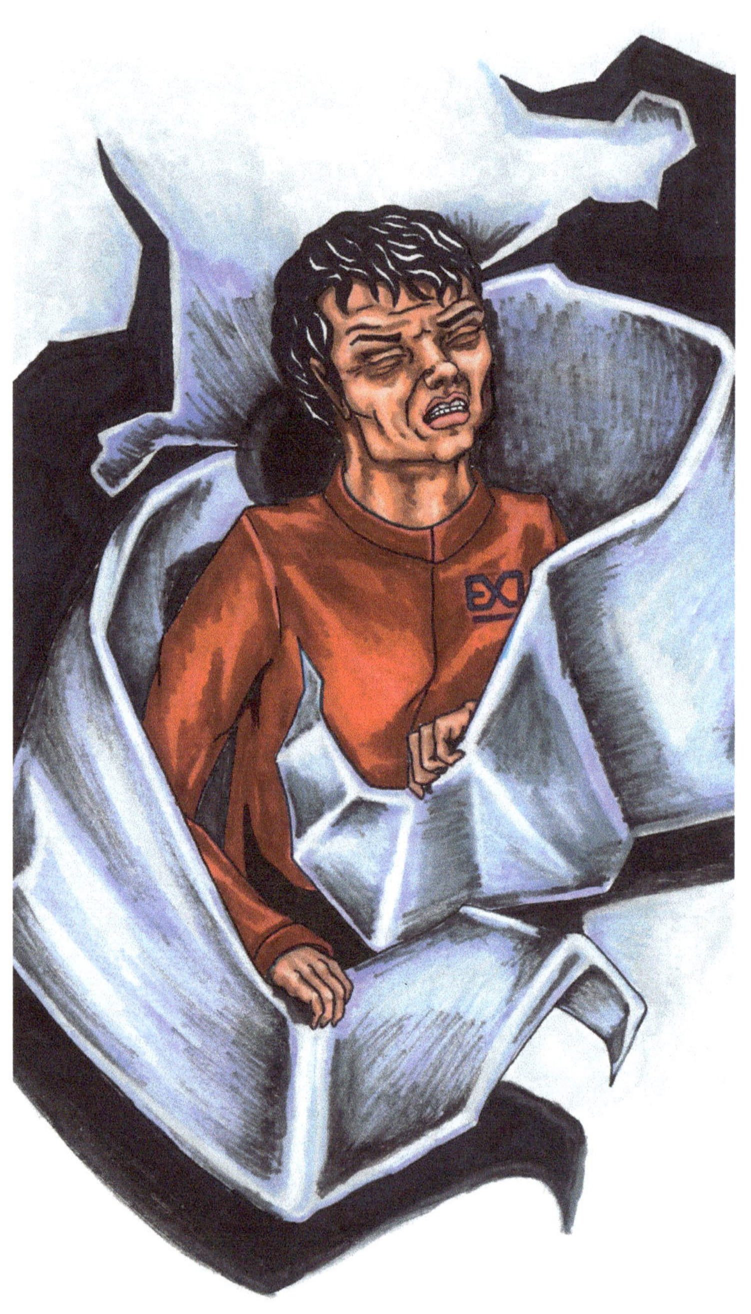

expected—more than Lincoln had really designed for in action. He fell forward against the soft blue wall, feeling very frail and very old.

Suddenly they were right there, laughing loudly just outside his bubble. Teeth clenched, Lincoln fought back the waves of emotion that pulsed down his body, each second dragging on like hours. He fought the emotion like he was part of the Stonewall Brigade, standing as tall as he could with just the power of his determination. Lincoln closed his eyes, trying to focus on their heavy steps so slowly moving away. Another wave of emotion came and he fought it like the 106th at the Bulge, digging in against the onslaught the best he could.

When he was sure they were gone, Lincoln fell to his knees and sobbed, wracked in uncontrollable grief.

It was the first time that he'd cried in a very long time. All of his emotions poured out now, in a great rush of release: it was sadness tinged with bitterness, but mostly an intensely deep feeling of loss—the loss of his sisters and brothers, all of his other friends, the young ones . . . but especially Helen. He cried for losing Helen most of all. Lincoln cried and cried and cried. He cried until the fog lifted from his brain. The cry was a liberation, seventy five some-odd years locked away. Lincoln cried until he was back in control of himself.

Afterwards, Lincoln still felt incredibly weak but better. Standing up slowly, the only way he could in the narrow chamber, he took a couple of deep breaths. It was very warm in there now, and the breaths condensed on the wall close to his face, a lingering blemish on the otherwise smooth surface. Taking one more deep breath, he stood proudly for a moment before changing the wall in front of him into a mirror. The change took the moisture with it.

The Captain assessed the damage with a frown. His face was streaked with tears, eyes red and irritated. Even his hair was out of shape. Working quickly, Lincoln wiped his face with his sleeves then used his hands to comb his hair back to its normal, impeccably neat state of affair. The water from his tears quickly evaporated off of his shirt, which looked as good as new. His eyes were still red but there was nothing to be done about that. Otherwise, Lincoln was satisfied with the image staring back at him.

No one but the Ship would know what had just happened.

A Poem from The Books of Bokonon

Tiger got to hunt,

Bird got to fly;

Man got to sit and wonder, "Why, why, why?"

Tiger got to sleep,

Bird got to land;

Man got to tell himself he understand.

Kurt Vonnegut
Cat's Cradle
Deceased 11 April 2007 AD (aged 84)
Manhattan, United States of America, Earth

NINE

Live for something. Do good, and
leave behind you a monument of
virtue that the storms of time can
never destroy. Write your name in
kindness, love, and mercy on the
hearts of thousands you come in
contact with year by year, and you
will never be forgotten.
Your name and your good deeds will
shine as the stars of heaven.

Thomas Chalmers
Deceased 31 May 1847 AD (aged 67)
Morningside, Kingdom of Great Britain, Earth

Lincoln was the last of his brothers and sisters to arrive at their private party near the core of the Ship. He was never late for anything, so this was a monstrous departure from decades of convention. They cheered sarcastically when the door slid open and he coolly tried to slide in like it was nothing.

It was a cozy room, set up with a shiny black rectangular table directly in the center and comfortable seats around it. Everyone was already sitting. One side of the room had a little bar area and a small enclosed hygiene chamber, the other a long, comfy couch. Virtually every inch of the wall space around them flashed with pictures and videos of the 8 of them, changing often in a colorful living collage: playing sports and games when they were kids, music recitals and other performances when they were a little older, dancing at past birthday parties, weddings, even formal doctoral presentations. There were a whole slew of candid shots too.

Music played from the walls:

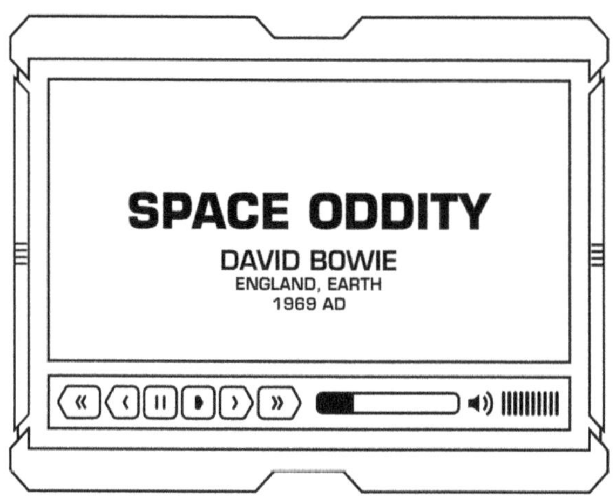

"Lincoln! Whatdidya get lost?" teased Ford. He was pretty hammered already. "Two times in one day! That's got to be some sorta record. You just ruined your average, brutha!"

Lincoln smiled broadly as he sat at his space at the table. "Hey, well—at least it's still better than yours."

Oz, seated next to him, leaned over and put his arm around Lincoln's shoulders. "You hungry, brother?"

"Yeah—a little," said Lincoln as it occurred to him. "I haven't eaten anything all day, except for Salkie's peppers of course." He turned to Salk. "Those, my friend, were very good. I'm proud of you."

"Thanks big bro," Salk replied with a smile.

"Best I could do in terms of snacks," said Emma, as she slid a sealed bowl of nuts and dried fruit down the table to Lincoln. "They were being real stingy in the kitchen…big birthday feast and all." With a left-handed hook shot she tossed him a fuzzy kiwi/plum.

Ford banged both fists on the table. "Those bastards! Don't they know that WE ARE GODS!"

They all laughed.

"A much better question … Link—do you wanna drink?"

The inadvertent rhyme cracked more laughter from Ford. He was clearly well on his way to what he and Lincoln used to (rather ignorantly) describe as a *memory-loss* night. Drunken overindulgence was never exemplary conduct, but right now it seemed as good an idea as any. Ford was serious about his ethanol, too. He poured a clear liquid from a large container into a cup, then mixed in liquids from two other smaller containers before passing the finished product down the line.

Lincoln raised his glass in a salute, making eye contact with each of them.

"Eat, drink, and be merry, my sisters and brothers, for tomorrow we die. I love you all so very much," he said.

"I love you," they all responded. "Love you too, Link!"

Lincoln slugged down a healthy gulp of Ford's dark concoction. It made him cough almost instantly. "That's some strong stuff," he said with a shake of his head and a smile.

Although their group was still bonded strongly by love, the four sisters and four brothers had grown further apart over the years—as usually happens. The exception, Emma, Dorothy and Oz had kept extremely tight. Emma had always been close with the couple, making the three of them a solid little clique for the last seventy seven some-odd years. Amelia and Ford, in contrast, had always possessed fierce streaks of independence. Not loners, per se (maybe Amelia to an extent, but certainly not Ford), both just stubbornly preferred to do things individually, off on their own adventures. Salk was your typical *bubblehead*, disappearing into his own world for long periods of time, and Lincoln had taken his Captaincy very seriously, which had pulled him in many different directions at once. Sojie, clearly always the mother of the bunch, was the glue that kept them all together. She played the part of the bridge, effortlessly spanning the various distances, keeping them all connected with that vital, loving gossip essential to keeping a family close.

"So . . ." asked Amelia with a cagey smile, "shall we?"

She looked around at them, looking regal in her beautiful, high-necked red dress, and now smiling rather cunningly. After a moment she became very serious. Then she looked directly at Dorothy, seated to her right, as she spoke.

"After all . . . there's no time to lose."

"Once upon a time . . ." Dorothy countered.

"In no time flat—" said Oz quickly.

"At the right place, at the right time," said Lincoln wisely.

"Art is long, and time is fleeting[8]," intoned Salk, earning more than a few groans.

"Footprints on the sands of time," said Emma, with a wrinkle of her nose at Salk.

"Time is limited!" declared Ford.

"I'm having the time of my life," said Sojourner with a wide smile.

With that the game began.

* * *

Every generation had their games, but the Zeta Alphas's had created a real doozy. Originally a much simpler concept stolen from somewhere else, it had evolved to become something quite different from what it was ever intended to be. To them, of course, it was pretty much the most amazing thing that had ever been invented.

The application was totally immersive; your eyes and ears playing the major roles, the environment around you constantly changing. It not only used your eye and ear implants in several different ways, but required a whole array of physical actions and gestures too. There were trivia rounds using movies and music, performances, puzzles of strategy and chance.

The rules? They'd developed so that there was a strict social hierarchy (entirely arbitrary, when it came down to it) starting immediately after the first challenge. Pretty soon, the game became ever-so detailed, with constantly updating points, credentials, and rankings, as well as the development of very onerous rules. The person at the top made all of the decisions, but most importantly what test of the mind or body to play next. *El Presidente* had control of all of the media used in every game, all the way down to the music playing in the background. Cheating was allowed—or at least accepted or ignored, depending on the situation. The people on top could blatantly ignore the rules, usually just rewriting them as the game went on. The people on the bottom, however, were punished severely if caught. The game never actually ended, either. Like some of the very first video games on Earth, you kept playing and playing and playing until you finally grew sick of it. Usually the Zeta Alpha's would give up only when a few of them quit, only after a long stretch of play. Sometimes that could be quite a long while.

The typical winning strategy at the top was to suppress those underneath you with just about every means possible, generally including alliances with others near the top, plus the use of gamesmanship and deception (all to the taste and moral compass of the person—Sojourner was a benevolent *Presidenta,* yet her rule never seemed to last very long). The typical winning strategy when not on the top was slow subversion, quietly amassing power, forming coalitions of all the weaker players to band together in a swooping moment of glory. If successful, the hierarchy could be upended. Then the game would plunge right back into a newly-mixed chaos of power moves and stupid rules. By nature, Amelia, Ford, and Lincoln had always been the competitors, with Emma and Salk also highly interested since they naturally loved games.

Today the game was very different though—it was way better! The Ship was in control of all the higher level decision making except for the mostly superficial (picking the music, for the most part, and sometimes setting the scene). The Ship made its choices so that the game was about the 8 of them. That was the only agenda. The media they watched and the music they heard were all of their favorites. The trivia was about them, composed of all of the moments in their lives from the mundane to the great.

"CHEATER!" several of them called while pointing at Ford, then laughing together. Smiling like a fox, Ford playfully hung his head in mock shame, knowing that he was caught and not giving a damn (currently directly at the bottom with nothing to lose).

They banged on the table, yelling out each other's names ... or phrases, or rhymes, or even random words. Sometimes they pointed at each other, or stood, or put their hands in the air. No matter what, the winner of each round danced happily at the end of it. They still fell into the same roles they'd taken as kids: Sojie the peace-keeper, known to be the only truly-trusted adjudicator in the game; Ford the instigator;

ever so impatient, Amelia always hurrying them up between rounds; Salk forever the inventor; Emma the mastermind, and never, ever, backing down from a fight; Dorothy and Oz always a team. The leaders were still the leaders, the followers were still the followers.

Lincoln became *el Presidente* for a short while in their now far more free-wheeling game. When he got the chance he toggled on a song and pumped up the volume. Soon, they were all singing it together as it blasted through the walls:

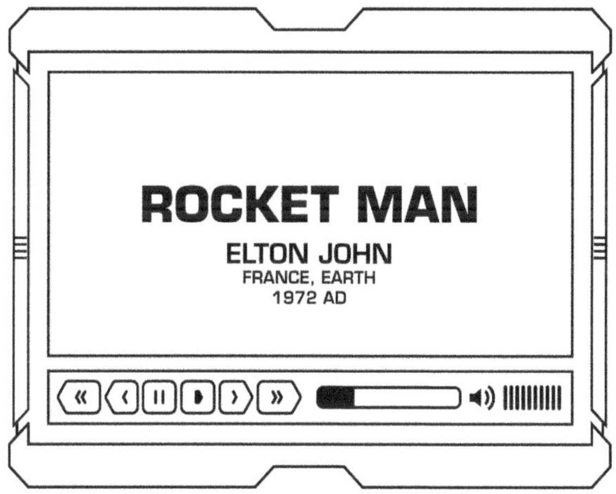

They continued to drink (all but Sojourner, who never did). As a matter of course they began to grow louder and louder as they got drunker and drunker, soon having the time of their lives. They pounded hard on the unrelenting black table. They popped up from their seats, sometimes one by one, or sometimes as a group, leaving the loser the only one sitting. They yelled at each other and often screamed in the air in frustration. Arms clinging to each other, they laughed and laughed and laughed.

After two and a half hours (which felt more like an hour if you'd asked them), the Ship gently lowered the music.

"Honorable Zeta Alpha generation . . ." the Ship spoke in each of their ears, in 8 separate voices. "The Lustrum Celebration has now fully assembled. Would you care to join everyone else at this time?"

They looked around at each other.

"I guess?" said Ford sarcastically.

"Let's do it," said Lincoln.

They all agreed.

Quite suddenly the walls of the room went black. The table began to slowly lower, the black material flowing like molten metal, seamlessly melding back into the black floor. Soon only the snack bowl and cups still left on the table remained in a broken circle on the floor, quickly claimed by their current owners. As they stood their seats also began to flow back into the floor, as well as the bar area and every other tangible object in the room. The brothers and sisters huddled together, forming a circle with their arms around one another.

This only lasted for a brief moment before the Ship

spoke again. "This way please, esteemed guests."

The easiest way to navigate your way through the ever-changing hallways of the Ship was simple: follow the white line. Through your eye implants, the Ship would direct your eyes along a path which only you could see. All you had to do was to follow the line being superimposed onto your vision. At that very moment, a heavy-duty white line appeared from the middle junction of two of the walls. The line slowly grew, moving horizontally across the wall. They all turned towards it, curiously tracking the movement. The white line soon crawled its way across the first wall and around to the next. Two walls bisected by a white line slowly became three. At the fourth wall the line terminated abruptly, directly in the middle. Then the wall shuddered, growing into a quiver, causing the group to hold their collective breath. Suddenly a bright sliver of light appeared at the bottom as the entire wall very slowly began to slide upwards.

In only a few breathless moments, in front of them was an absolutely cavernous room filled with music and laughter, containing the entire human population of the Ship. At first the mass of people was not aware of the small group huddled in what was essentially a tiny alcove in a small section of one wall, but the surprise of the people closest to them quickly turned a smattering of hoots and hollers into thunderous, sustained applause as the guests of honor were received by their community. It wasn't just the sound that was palpable, either (though it was just about the loudest thing any of them had ever heard). It was the energy of the room, too: waves of vibrations from vocal cords, clapping and stomping of hands and feet, in addition to the heat and vitality of the people and the smell of good food.

Almost too much to take in, time seemed to slow.

Still huddled close together, the Zeta Alphas didn't seem to know what to do until two of the ten-year-olds broke from the crowd towards them. A boy and girl dressed simply in white ran forward, laughing, before taking Sojourner by the hands and ushering her back into the crowd, where she was almost instantly enveloped. Next, Salk was greeted by an awkward trio of younger scientists and led in the direction of many more. Captain Kennedy slowly emerged from the crowd next, certainly looking the part: tall, dapper and handsome. He surprised Lincoln by walking right past him and up to Ford, then vigorously shaking his brother's hand with both of his own and leading him into the crowd. Smiling at one another and with a collected shrug, Emma, Oz, and Dorothy grabbed hands and walked themselves out into the crowd. Seeing that, and with a similar shrug, Amelia walked towards the throng on her own, her head held high. Hedy, her supposed escort, met her at the edge of the throng, shaking her head admiringly with a huge smile.

This left Lincoln standing there by himself.

Then he saw her. Slowly emerging from the crowd was Helen, the people around her parting like she was the goddess Venus emerging from the ocean. Helen looked stunning, as beautiful as she'd ever been. Her dark hair, held up high, framed her face but particularly her piercing, violet eyes, which were further accentuated with the black make-up around them. Her lips were painted deep red. But the most striking feature was her dress. It certainly wasn't the dress she'd shown him a week ago—the custom-designed, sophisticated red number. The dress Helen wore was white, shimmering iridescently, with a brilliant silver thread looped several times around her thin waist. All else was shaped by Helen herself. A bright jewel adorned her chest, creating a pattern of light that sparkled across her bodice before forming long, flowing streams of white lightning that followed the length of fabric to her feet.

Helen was wearing a wedding dress, it dawned on Lincoln, and a stunning one at that. *She must have changed her plans right after the luncheon!* As his lover gracefully approached him, the movement of the fine fabric below her knees shimmered, glistening as if wet. The effect made it look like Helen was walking on a cloud.

They locked eyes, and Lincoln followed her violet orbs until she was standing directly in front of him. The fragrance Helen wore was somehow both heavenly and exotic, and he closed his eyes as she snuggled close to his chest, grabbing hold of his hands with hers. They stayed this way for a few precious moments until she tugged him, softly turning and guiding Lincoln towards the rest of their people.

Plunging into the crowd was a maelstrom of faces and noises and smells. Lincoln was instantly enveloped by a very large circle waiting to pay their respects. He was plied with hugs and kisses and so many kind words, stories of shared adventures and valuable lessons learned. He saw his oldest friends and all of his many mentees, including all of the other Captains. *The oldest statesmen of the group for not much longer,* he noticed.

Even the fifteen-year-olds were patiently waiting for him together. It was rapid fire, the gameshow bonus round, one person right after another, conversation after conversation, each one frustratingly cut short by the next. Helen was with him the whole time, the ballast to his sail, helping to hold Lincoln steady against the onslaught of attention. It took some time to work their way over, but she unwaveringly guided them towards the long tables filled with all manners of colorful foods. Helen knew what Lincoln liked best and took control, filling his plate with all of his favorites while he was still occupied by other loved ones. She made sure that he ate, then refilled their plates again. They washed their food down with gulps of smooth wine, the grapes of the vintage harvested eighty years ago to the day.

The hours passed quickly in a dizzying mix of fun. There was a break in the conversations a little later, the lights suddenly dimming. Captain Kennedy took the small stage and quickly introduced the first prepared speaker, Hedy, Zeta Gamma, an old friend of theirs. The great wall behind the stage lit up like an old-style movie marquee with:

Pictures and videos flashed on all walls as the tribute began, often changing exactly with Hedy's words as she began to describe her idol. Amelia was fondly known as a strong, independent, butt-kicking woman, and there were many examples of this shown in appreciation—much to the delight of the crowd.

Following Amelia, the rest of the sisters and brothers were each celebrated in different manners. Some of the multi-media presentations were solo acts, some tag-team affairs. Sometimes the speeches were small roasts with lots of humor, recounting hilarious stories, but each and every presentation had an extremely heart-felt delivery at the end of it. Sojourner's was especially emotional; a well-rehearsed little play put on by all of the ten-year-olds.

The presentations each began with a personal headline emblazoned across the wall of the stage:

SALK /sawk, sawlk
noun: A tireless clinical technician
and man with true honor and integrity

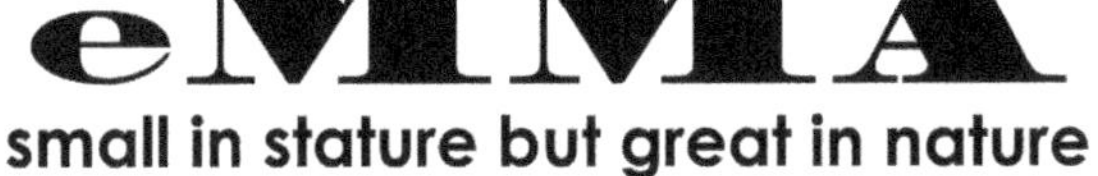

LINCOLN:
THE STRONGEST MAN I HAVE EVER KNOWN

Mother Sojourner's tireless love for everyone else.

After the wonderful presentations, many types of musicians performed; voices and instruments combining in soaring, virtuosic displays that brought goose bumps to the arms and legs. The trained dancers took over the center of the room for some time as the music heated up—most leaving little to nothing to the imagination in terms of clothes, and ringed by circles of hooting people encouraging them on. At one point, and to everyone's utmost delight, it was only Helen and Lincoln in the center. Helen laughed as Lincoln playfully tried to mimic some of the moves he'd just seen, then she showed everyone who was boss of the dance floor.

As the party continued a fragrance emerged; perspiration mixed with the food and the booze. Kisses became longer—and significantly saltier. The dance floor pulsed, the thundering bass growing until it drowned out much of everything else. The dancing became less inhibited and more primal, movements more and more exaggerated. Lincoln and Helen danced together like when they were young, the music and the energy of the people around them guiding their movements. Drunk and happy, Lincoln was in the moment, enjoying Helen and finally able to enjoy himself.

But all too soon the heavy beat faded away and the Ship's most famous melody began. It was a slow, plaintive song with a prolonged build-up, carefully performed by the woman widely regarded as the greatest living singer on the Ship. This, their swan song, was a derivative; its value much greater than the sum of its parts. The lyrics had been from an ancient poem before a songwriter had finally woven them into the emotional melody that the woman now sang, building the story slowly:

> *Because I could not stop for death*
> *he kindly stopped for me.*
> *The carriage held but just ourselves*
> *and immortality.*
>
> *We slowly drove, he knew no haste.*
> *I put away my labor, leisure and fun.*

There were no more places I could run.

We passed the school where
children played,
their lessons scarcely done,
We passed the fields of gazing grain.

We passed the setting sun.
We passed the setting sun.
We passed the setting sun.

Or, rather, she passed us.
The dews drew quivering and chill.
For only gossamer my blanket had
become.

We paused before a house that seemed
A swelling of the ground.
The roof was scarcely visible,
The cornice but a mound.

We passed the setting sun.
We passed the setting sun.
We passed the setting sun.

Since then, tis centuries, and yet feels
shorter than the day
I first surmised the horses' heads
were toward eternity.

We passed the setting sun.
We passed the setting sun.
We passed the setting sun. [9]

The music in diminuendo, the crowd was quiet, slowly swaying together, some of the vibrant energy just in the room seeming to dissipate. Helen's grip on Lincoln became more and more vise-like as they danced closely, clearly affected by the song. She held his hand but also wrapped her other arm around him tightly. Helen was the one who needed the support now. Softly, she began to sob into his shirt.

The clock hit midnight and the great gong of a bell rang out, struck just once but reverberating for many seconds as the lights slowly dimmed. Basked in spotlights that twinkled into existence like stars at dusk, a piece of wall rose up revealing another small room. The crowd coalesced into a hot, smelly mass that surrounded Lincoln and his brothers and sisters. Soon the circle broke with a single opening that faced the new alcove.

Lincoln stood stoically while Helen's crying intensified.

Captain Kennedy paced to the space in front of the alcove, his hands clenched in front of him solemnly. His intonation was serious:

"Distinguished Zeta Alpha generation, your accomplishments have been celebrated. Each of you has touched many others. You have lived great lives, and we will remember what you have taught us. We send you out with all of the love and honor that you deserve."

The current Captain bowed deeply.

"May the rest of your journeys be peaceful."

With that, Kennedy moved out of the way. Applause rose, though more reserved than before; a dignified exit, as opposed to the raucous entrance they'd received hours earlier.

Lincoln looked down at Helen. Her face was buried in his chest, her tears creating a large wet patch on his shirt. She shook like a leaf in a November storm, holding on to him for dear life. Lincoln closed his eyes and exhaled loudly before he spoke gently to her.

"Helen, my love. It's time…" He shook her ever so slightly. "You need to let go. It will be okay, but you have to let me go."

Tears welled in his eyes but Lincoln somehow managed to hold it together.

Slowly her grip relaxed, until she finally let go of him completely. She stood, hunched over, her tears streaming down uncontrollably as she wept. He put his arms around her one last time.

"Words cannot express what you have meant to

me, Helen," he whispered to her. "You are an amazing woman, and you have made me so very happy. I love you more than I could ever express."

With that, Lincoln released her. He kissed both of her wet cheeks one last time and turned. His generation was standing before him, all holding hands. Sojourner reached out and Lincoln took his place at the end of the line. As a group, they turned and walked towards the small room, to sustained applause.

Glancing backwards as he was pulled, Lincoln saw that Helen still stood by herself, totally wracked with grief. That's when he sent her something which he'd spent weeks composing. It was the only love letter he'd ever written, written just for now.

The small room they entered was empty, with the typical obsidian black floor, but with textured walls that glittered like white marble. The brightness of the room coupled with the spotlights beyond the doorway made the crowd disappear into relative darkness. With a shudder, the door slowly began to close, the applause swelling audibly for one moment more. When the door finally sealed closed with a great WHOOSH, a good amount of the air in the room seemed to go out with it.

For a moment, it was as silent and dark as any tomb found anywhere.

TEN

All forms that perish other forms supply,
(By turns we catch the vital breath and die)
Like bubbles on the sea of matter borne,
They rise, they break, and to that sea return.

Alexander Pope
Deceased 30 May 1744 AD (aged 56)
Twickenham, Kingdom of Great Britain, Earth

The dim white light that grew from the ceiling did nothing against the cold in the small room. For some reason, none of them thought to change the fact. Someone did bring up a long black bench from the floor and a few of them sat. Others stood, wearily leaning against the walls. All except for Sojourner were pretty drunk at that point—a good way to go out, according to Ship consensus. They were all disheveled: hair untidied, clothes wet, wrinkled and smelly, eyes red.

"You know . . ." slurred Ford, by far the drunkest. "The condemned gotta last meal back on 'Urth. Cheeseburger and fries. Apple pie, alamo. Waffles! Shiiiite … just about anything you could think of. Serial killer on death row? Sure. Here ya go sir, steak and fava beans—bloody as hell, just like you like it! Child rapist? Hello there Father Thomas, here's all the candy you could possibly eat in one sitting AND some medicine for that tummy ache."

"Ford," Amelia interrupted tiredly, "what's the point?"

"The point—my dear sister—is that after all this time you woulda thought the esteemed *homo evolutish* woulda managed something better for a last meal! I mean, I have no idea what a burger actually tastes like. Neither do you. But I bet Salkie could make a pretty darn good one outa algae if he wanted …"

Salk nodded confidently at this.

"Then commission grains from the farms for bread, and the pie crust, cook up apples with sugar. It's all possible … it's just chemistry! But all we get for a last meal is the same old vegan crap we always get— just more of it."

He looked around at their blank, tired stares.

"We can do better is the point!" Ford resolved with a huff.

The room lapsed back into silence.

After some time another wall slowly slid open with a rumble, still maintaining the marble motif, revealing a threshold that led down a long, dark corridor. Those seated now stood, and the bench flowed back into the floor. Amelia was the first to the threshold.

She was almost through it when Salk spoke.

"Hey! Wait a second! We came in together. We should go out together."

He grabbed her hand. Dorothy grabbed his hand and soon they remade the chain, just like when they were kids: Amelia and Salk and Dorothy and Oz and Emma and Ford and Sojourner. Lincoln was at the end of the line again, out of character; the caboose, twice in a matter of minutes.

Her head held high, Amelia led them across the threshold into the darkness. Yet as they entered, lights began to flick on, making the long hallway almost blindingly bright and warm compared to where they had just been. At the end was another dark portal. It was only after they had cleared this door that they knew that they were now in the Medical Ward, the large, clinically white space close to where Sojourner and Lincoln had stood only hours before.

Slowly, 8 empty black tables rose up from the floor in a line.

Amelia broke the chain and walked to the furthest table. She stood in front of it proudly, somehow still looking regal despite it all. Her brothers and sisters followed suit. This left Lincoln as the last one to take a position in front of a table.

Lincoln felt eerily composed. It was bizarre, given all that he'd gone through in all of the time leading up to this moment. All of the anguish. All of the questions, seeking answers which were never there, plus all of those sleepless nights, and being tired all the time. But today had been so packed with activity that there hadn't been any time to fixate on death, or anything else. Now, at the end, the stress had dissipated. All of the things that had so bothered him before were nothing more than a bad dream which had faded away.

The Ship spoke through the walls in a gentle voice.

"This is the easy part, my dear friends. As you lay down I will prime the final order in your brain implants. When you close your eyes for a few seconds, you will fall asleep. That's it. Like I said…really easy."

Amelia hopped up on her table, scooting backwards.

"Wait—that's it!?!" Sojourner scolded. "You're always in such a rush, love. At least give your sister one more hug!"

Obliging with a smile, Amelia hopped off the table as Sojourner rushed to her. They met with a bear hug. Soon everyone was embracing, saying goodbye to each another with hugs and kisses and final words. It was a distinguished thing[10], a somber goodbye; the elements of the clinical environment, the hour, and the morbid deed itself naturally causing them to speak in hushed voices, afraid to pierce the pervading quiet.

When they were done with their goodbyes they once again took up their positions. This time they hopped up on the tables at the same time, scooting backwards and lying together synchronously, as if on cue. They had been trained well, after all.

As she lay, Sojourner reached out both hands in opposite directions. Ford took one hand and Lincoln took the other. The chain was reestablished once more.

"Good night, Amelia ..." called Sojourner.

"Good night, Sojourner," Amelia answered. "Good night Oz and Dorothy. Good Night Salk. Good night Emma. Good night Ford. Good night Lincoln."

Each said goodbye to one another aloud, by name. The buzz of voices rose for a brief moment, echoing lively throughout the small room. Yet too soon it became quiet again.

"Are we ready?" asked Ford tiredly, breaking the stillness, drunk and numb to it all. Sojourner squeezed Lincoln's hand. He squeezed back as he took a deep breath.

"It was good to know you, Captain Lincoln," the

seductive female voice of the Ship spoke in his ear. "I promise that I will never forget you."

A baby in the nursery next door began to scream, almost as if on cue. It was the hysterical cry of a newborn demanding something. Time seemed to slow, the babe's cries growing deeper, stretched-out like the Ship was traveling through the event horizon of a black hole.

Lincoln took three slow, steadying deep breaths before sighing audibly once. Then he closed his eyes.

Was I who I set out to be? was the very last thing he thought.

You couldn't tell it at first, but Captain Lincoln was dead.

O Captain! My Captain!

O Captain! my Captain! our fearful trip is done,
The ship has weather'd every rack, the prize we sought is won,
The port is near, the bells I hear, the people all exulting,
While follow eyes the steady keel, the vessel grim and daring;
But O heart! heart! heart!
O the bleeding drops of red,
Where on the deck my Captain lies,
Fallen cold and dead.

O Captain! my Captain! rise up and hear the bells;
Rise up—for you the flag is flung—for you the bugle trills,
For you bouquets and ribbon'd wreaths—for you the shores
a-crowding,
For you they call, the swaying mass, their eager faces turning;
Here Captain! dear father!
This arm beneath your head!
It is some dream that on the deck,
You've fallen cold and dead.

My Captain does not answer, his lips are pale and still,
My father does not feel my arm, he has no pulse nor will,
The ship is anchor'd safe and sound, its voyage closed and
done,
From fearful trip the victor ship comes in with object won;
Exult O shores, and ring O bells!
But I with mournful tread,
Walk the deck my Captain lies,
Fallen cold and dead.

Walt Whitman
Deceased 26 March 1892 AD (aged 72)
Camden, United States of America, Earth

NOTES

[1] Alan Seeger, "I Have a Rendezvous with Death" (1917 AD). This poem was a particular favorite of President John F. Kennedy.

[2] Elisabeth Kübler-Ross, *"On Death and Dying,"* (1969 AD). Kübler-Ross was a pioneer in understanding the problems caused by the medicalization of death. "The more we are making advances in science," she wrote, "the more we seem to fear and deny the reality of death." In Atul Gawade's Being Mortal: Medicine and What Happens in the End, (2014) she observed that a terminal patient "may cry for rest, peace, and dignity, but he will get infusions, transfusions, a heart machine."

[3] Irving Berlin, "Blue Skies." (1926 AD).

[4] Sigmund Freud, "Future of an Illusion." (1927 AD).

[5] Henry Beston, The Outermost House: A Year of Life On The Great Beach of Cape Cod (1928 AD).

[6] The incomparable Professor Carl Sagan in Cosmos episode #13 (PBS, 1980 AD): "Every culture on the planet has devised its own response to the riddle of the Universe. There are many different ways of being

human. But an extra-terrestrial visitor examining the differences among human societies would find those differences trivial compared to the similarities. We are one species. We are star-stuff, harvesting starlight. Our past and our future are tied to the sun, the moon and the stars."

7 Walt Whitman, Leaves of Grass (1892 AD).

8 Henry Wadsworth Longfellow, A Psalm of Life (1838 AD).

9 Emily Dickinson, "Because I could not stop for death" (1890 AD).

10 Writer Henry James on his deathbed (1916 AD): "So here it is at last, the distinguished thing."

ABOUT THE ARTIST

Kimberly Hazen is a woman whose path in life has been forged based on her undying drive to create something where there was nothing. She currently resides in New Orleans, USA, Earth.

There are many arguments over the definition of the term Art. What defines Art? Why are there these invisible lines between Art and craft, or indeed, Art and garbage? Kimberly Hazen believes that Art is simply bigger than these definitions. She is of the mind that the ability to see beyond the parts is what makes an Artist. To see a piece of paper or a lump of clay, and see its true potential. To take seemingly useless things and turn them into something more, something meaningful, something that invokes the senses of others.

As time progresses it may be this artistic mindset that saves mankind. Perhaps in this great abyss there is a speck, so far and insignificant that most wouldn't take a second look. But someone with the ability to see something where others see nothing may turn an eye to that rock, and see a future where there was none, see salvation, see Home.

ABOUT THE AUTHOR

EXO Books is the pen name and publishing company of a science fiction writer. He is a man who lives in New York City, USA, Earth.

The name EXO Books was inspired from the book of Exodus in the Bible. An exodus is the departure of a people out of slavery, to a promised land. It is a journey punctuated with peaks and valleys of joy and sorrow, through darkness ever towards the light. Inherent to this great journey of ours is the notion that while we continue to search for a better life, this search may not be fruitful in our individual lifetimes. Still, we try. Through it all we are sustained by our love for each other, and by hope.

The road is long, my friends. We trek on together.